COLLATERAL DAMAGE

Miski Harris

Heaven's Scent PUBLISHING

This book is a work of fiction. Names, characters, places, and incidents either are products of the author's imagination or are used fictitiously. Any resemblance to actual events or locales or persons, living or dead, is entirely coincidental.

Copyright 2020 by Miski Harris

All rights reserved, including the right of reproduction in whole or in part in any form.

Published by Heaven Scent's Publishing

Formatting by Kris Jacen

Issued 2020

This book is licensed to the original purchaser only. Duplication or distribution via any means is illegal and a violation of International Copyright Law, subject to criminal prosecution and upon conviction, fines and/or imprisonment. This eBook cannot be legally loaned or given to others. No part of this eBook can be shared or reproduced without the express permission of the publisher

ACKNOWLEDGEMENTS

There is nothing in this world like having that one ride-or-die friend who will always have your back. For me that friend is Amy Wasp-Wimberger. You have been my greatest supporter during those dark moments when I wasn't sure life was even worth it. You reached out and shared with me, not from an abundance but from within your own personal lack. We laughed, we cried, and we pulled each other through some crazy times. I will always be ever grateful for your love and undying support. I hope *Collateral Damage* makes you proud.

Tammy Stephens: You laughed when I said I needed a keeper, but you took the job on anyway. You literally put my name on the map, and "thank you" just doesn't seem to be enough.

Taffy Schunter Thomas: You have been the best beta any author could ask for. I will never in a million years be able to thank you enough for all your hard work keeping me on track, encouraging me when I got stuck, and most of all, the endless hours of reading and re-reading to help me tell Jordan's story his way.

A special thanks to Emmy Ellis, the artistic talent behind this awe-inspiring cover. I will be ever grateful for your decision to finish the series.

Last but not least to Kris Jacen for the innumerable hours you put into the re-edit and formatting of this book to make it into the story I worked so hard to tell.

AUTHOR'S NOTE

Ron, Troy, Demitri, Benny, Mikey and Angel; the service dogs Sweetie and Poochie; Vincent's restaurant; the town of Red Deer, Colorado, the surrounding Rocky Mountain Foothills areas of interest and entertainment all appear with the permission and cooperation of their creator A.E. Wasp from her Veterans Affairs Series. Any resemblance to existing towns, and attractions is purely the result of our combined imaginations and the love I developed for the area during my short stay there.

Loveland, Colorado is a real place and its claim to fame lies in activities like that described in this book.

The U.S. Military and the Department of Veterans Affairs Medical Services have a long history in Colorado. Together they serve and meet the needs of uncounted veterans every year.

Post-traumatic stress disorder (PTSD) is a mental health condition that's triggered by either a physical or mental event. The flashbacks, nightmares and severe anxiety, as well as uncontrollable thoughts about the event create a storm in the life of the sufferer that can be unbearable.

I want to dedicate this book to all my veteran brothers and sisters who have met this storm and are pushing through for their personal victories on the other side of it.

The struggle is real.

To My husband Thomas

7/12/1948 – 2/10/2019

You not only read *Don't Ask Don't Tell*, but you also bragged about it to everyone whether they wanted to hear it or not. I hope *Collateral Damage* makes you just as proud.

Sleep in Peace

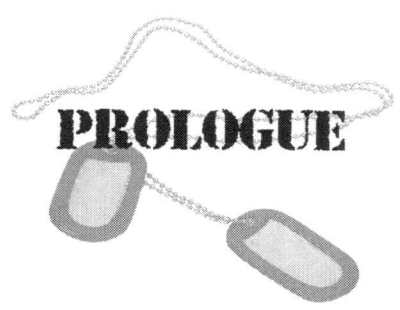

PROLOGUE

March 1998

Sergeant Jordan Washington entered the barracks' common room of his dormitory. The usual group of noisy airmen lounged around on the various generic couches and chairs, watching television or playing cards or board games. What was different was the unusual number of men grouped together having a loud, angry-sounding discussion that came to a halt as he entered the room. No one spoke, but the sudden silence told him everything he needed to know. He was once again the topic of discussion. The new pariah. No one knew exactly what happened to EJ, their friend and teammate. All they knew was he was gone quicker than a fart in the wind, and they were all certain old iron-lips Jordan knew why and was refusing to say.

Jordan continued through the common room to the darkened hallway his room was located in. He massaged his temples in an attempt to alleviate the headache threatening to further fuck up his day. *Funny. When it's their secrets I'm keeping, I'm the man of the hour. But now I'm the unit bitch. Why the fuck did I accept the transfer to this job in the first place? Because, jackass, you were tired of being on alert all the time but unable to join the fellas where the real action was. You needed time to heal and rehabilitate without endangering your chances of returning to the team.*

As much as Jordan hated to admit it, even to himself, staying on Kadena as an admin served that purpose.

He halted in front of his room door and pressed his forehead to the cool, hard, wood door. He'd left his office feeling lower than he'd felt since the day he said goodbye to EJ at base ops for the last time. He'd not heard from his friend since. He wondered what had happened to him and what he decided to do.

So, what have I got now? The unit commander's gone. EJ is gone. The wing is in an uproar and everyone is looking at me. When we tally the cost of destruction, nobody ever considers the collateral damage.

"How the fuck did this shit suddenly fall on my shoulders?" he asked aloud to the empty hallway.

"The same way it always does, Jordy," said a soft whisper in the darkness.

"Richard? What are you doing here?"

"I need to talk to you."

Technical Sargent Richard Morgan, Jordan's old combat search and rescue team leader, sauntered into Jordan's field of vision. Jordan couldn't help but admire the fine specimen of man standing in front of him: jet-black hair, ocean-blue eyes, and five foot ten inches of well-defined muscles, the kind gotten from combining working out with hard work. Richard would never be a gym bunny, that was for sure. Jordan salivated and his dick hardened slightly as he recalled the long, thick, uncut member that lay beneath Richard's uniform like the concealed weapon it was. Then, he just as quickly remembered the painful cost of his one night with the walking wet dream. Richard's tastes ran a bit kinky for Jordan, and he didn't bottom—ever.

Too bad his insides didn't match the outside, Jordan thought as he surveyed temptation on legs. He could really use a good, long, hot night without having to think.

Yeah right. You want to explain to Michael how you made yet another mistake?

Snapping out of his musings, he looked up to see Richard had moved behind him, invading his personal space by placing on hand on the door near Jordan's head. Richard's body was so close, all he had to do was move one inch closer and those lips would be on Jordan.

Jordan turned to put his key in the lock. "What the hell do you think you're doing here? Half the squadron is in the fucking dayroom."

"Then open the damn door, boy, and we'll have all the privacy we need," Richard commanded, showing a slow, leering smile.

If it were possible, Jordan was sure his face would be as red as a ripe tomato. "Boy! If I've told you once, Richard, I've told you a thousand times. I am not now, nor will I ever be, your boy, or sub, or whatever the fuck it is you call it. Take that weird shit down the road, son. Now. What the hell do you want?"

His hands up in surrender, Richard took two steps back. "Easy, babe. I came here on important business. I have to leave in the morning, so just hear me out."

With a resigned sigh, Jordan unlocked the door to his room and admitted Richard. Richard could be an ass, but he was also not a man to waste time. So, if he only had one day on island and he was standing in front of Jordan, it had to be important.

Richard walked in and looked around the barrack room as if for the first time. The single bed pristinely dressed only with the issued linens and a woolen blanket sat along one wall, with a plain wooden desk that had clearly seen better days adjacent to it. The single wide chest of drawers was positioned across from the bed. The only nonissue pieces of furniture were the full-length butler mirror that sported a storage drawer at its base, and the thirty-two-inch color TV on the chest, strategically turned to face the bed.

"Love what you've done with the place. I hear basic military chic is all the rage these days," Richard said wryly while taking a seat on the lone chair in front of the desk.

"Did you come here to talk to me or advise me on how to redecorate my room?" Jordan asked as he pulled a beer and a Coke out of the small fridge that sat near the foot of his bed. "Talk fast. The colonel's called a meeting and I'm expected to be there."

Taking the beer from Jordan, Richard let out a laugh. "I thought those meetings were for officers and senior enlisted only."

"Normally they are, but I got a message that my attendance was required, so hurry up and speak your piece."

"Okay, but since when do you drink pop after duty instead of a beer? You been visiting BC Street and need to abstain till you finish your meds?"

"You know, you really should reenlist. You'll never make it as a comedian. I told you the colonel sent me my own en-damn-graved invite. You think it wise I show up with beer on my breath? You said you have a point to make. Make it. Fast!"

Taking a deep drink of his beer, Richard continued. "We've never permanently filled your spot on the team. I told the chief I'd see if you were ready to come back. I know you miss it, Jordy. There is no way in hell you're gonna convince me you prefer playing secretary to that lazy lard ass you work for."

"You act like it's so simple." Jordan sighed. "You're right. I miss it, and I know what happened wasn't my fault. Thing is, suppose it happens again? I may not be able to handle it."

Richard set his beer on the floor by his chair, walked over to Jordan and placed both hands on his shoulders. "You're not handling it now. Here's the thing. It happens to someone every damn day, man. It's part of the job. They told you on day one that you can't and won't save everyone. All you can do is get out there and try. Right now, there are people alive today because you were on duty."

Richard slowly walked to the window of the drab room and pressed his hands down hard against the sill. He took a deep breath, then turned to face Jordan, his eyes blazing. "Listen, bitch.

You and I both know your leg is fine and the only reason you are malingering in this mindless job is because you have the flight surgeon convinced that you're still not ready to jump qualify."

Moving once again in front of Jordan, Richard reached down and grabbed him by the top of his shirt, pulling him to his feet. "Admit it, motherfucker. You're still brooding over what happened on that rescue, and you've convinced yourself you're no longer any good. Well, I call bullshit. I tell you what. Jump quals are in two days. You test and fail, I'll shut the fuck up and you can go on playing Ms. March to whatever candy ass they put in the base CO's chair. Deal is, you give me your word that you will do your best. If you pass like I know you will, you man up and suit up."

Jordan peeled Richard's hand from his shirt. He knew if he took Richard up on his deal, he'd pass the eval and be back in a flight suit quicker than you could say "Gear up." He'd been physically combat-ready for ages. He'd been unsure of himself just as long.

Letting out the deep breath he hadn't realized he'd been holding, he dropped his head. "Deal," he said softly.

"Not good enough. Look me in the eye and say it like you mean it."

Raising his head and facing Richard, his eyes burning with a determination he didn't quite feel inside, Jordan said, "Deal! Now can I please relax before this meeting? The colonel is pissed, and I for one would like to fly a little more below his radar."

Opening the door, Richard turned to leave but stopped for one last comment. "Here's some food for thought, Jordan. Come home where you belong, and you'll be so far below his radar, his next phrase will be 'Jordan who?'" Laughing at his own joke, Richard closed the door quickly, avoiding the book Jordan threw at him, which landed with a dull thud on the polished wooden floor.

• • •

At six feet five inches tall, Colonel Williams was an imposing figure no matter how he dressed. Like many airmen, when in his dress uniform, he seemed to walk taller, fiercer, and frankly looked straight-out terrifying. When the man was angry, his hazel eyes seemed to turn storm gray. Those who had been exposed to it said his I-am-truly-pissed look could literally stop time. With the stealth of a panther, Colonel Wilson walked in through the backdoor of the multipurpose room and was halfway to the front before a master sergeant noticed him and called the room to attention.

He strode straight to the podium, where he placed his leather-bound notepad already open to the points he planned to make. Giving a surveying glance around the packed room of senior noncommissioned officers and officers of all grades, he asked, "Can someone tell me how this command lost the most talented avionics technician we've had since the weapons were introduced into the inventory? My understanding is there isn't enough money in the federal mint or promotions in the Air Force to convince him to reenlist and return."

From the back of the room, a young second lieutenant spoke up with a slow drawl, alluding to Southern roots. "Weelll, suh, he can't come back. He's gay." Ignoring the attempts of the men around him to shut him up, he tried to continue. "I mean—"

Colonel Williams cut him off. "I don't give a merry damn how happy he is. We didn't ask—he didn't tell. My understanding is his unit commander took advantage of his position of leadership until the shit hit the fan. Then the command parties involved tried to roll an Article 125 bus over Staff Sergeant Jackson. It might have worked if he'd been anyone else."

The lieutenant, who clearly had more nerve than brains, continued to try to press his point. "Suh, that's not quite the story we heard."

Colonel Williams looked at the small contingent of men trying without success to hush the arrogant man and said, "You men step aside. Get up here, Lieutenant Miles."

A slim figure, sharply dressed in battle camouflage and spotless boots, walked up to the front of the room and cockily positioned himself in front of the podium.

A look of disbelief crossed Colonel Williams's face. The man in front of him appeared barely out of puberty. His uniform was so new, you could still smell the clothing-issue stabilizer that permeated uniforms purchased and not yet washed. Turning his steely gray gaze on the lieutenant, Colonel Williams spoke in a low, terse voice that didn't bode well for the young idiot standing in front of him like he had the world by the tail.

"Where the hell are you from, boy?"

"LaFollette, Tennessee, suh," replied the proud-looking young man.

Colonel Williams abandoned his position to stand nose-to-nose with the arrogant young man. Speaking in a controlled way, enunciating each word carefully, he said, "So let me get this straight, Miles. You traveled over twelve thousand miles just to piss me the fuck off?"

Finally getting a clue, Miles' proud posture diminished as he quietly uttered, "No, suh."

"I don't really give a damn what you heard. We are airmen, not a bunch of damn fishwives. We work, fly, and fight as one." Stepping closer, Colonel Williams looked the chastised young lieutenant in the eyes. "So, in spite of what you think you heard, the only story that counts and the only one I ever want to hear is the story you're hearing now," he bit out, once again at a full boil. "With one exception, all parties directly involved in this maddening mess are off the base, and we are going to work our asses off to regain our stellar reputation of unbreakable teamwork. Any questions?"

"No, suh," replied Miles.

"Good. As for the rest of you, anytime I can get wind of the bullshit going on in the barracks concerning who knew what and how, things have gone too far. We eat, sleep, and shit as a team. Since I believe the speed of the group reflects the speed of the leadership, the change starts in this room. Any questions?"

The men and women assembled responded shook their collective heads.

Satisfied his point had been made, Colonel Wilson returned his attention to the matter of what to do with the smartass lieutenant. The colonel was well known for making the punishment fit the crime, and the decision he suddenly came to was perfect.

"Chief Chenault, front and center."

Chief Master Sergeant Chenault approached the podium. He shook his head slowly as he made his way forward, parting the men and women in front of him. The quiet laughter in the room was confirmation that men and women were happy it was him and not them. Because the last thing any senior NCO in the room needed or wanted was some green-behind-the-ears lieutenant to train.

"Settle down, people," Colonel Wilson said in a voice that brooked no disobedience. "Chief, I want you to meet Lieutenant Jackass. Until further notice, he is assigned to you for remedial training in human relations. I am trusting you to show him the error of his ways and to inform him on what will become his new leadership style."

Returning to the podium as Chief Chenault and the now thoroughly chastised Gordan Miles returned to their seats, Colonel Wilson consulted his notes. "One last thing. I never again in my time here want to hear of the base commander or anybody else being so directly involved in wing affairs. If any of you idiots are confused about the way the chain of command works, grab one of your lower enlisted troops and have them give you a refresher." Looking around the room once again, he spotted the man he was looking for. "Sergeant Washington, with me, now!"

Wasting no time, Jordan rose and moved quickly to the podium, then strode swiftly behind Colonel Williams as he exited the room.

• • •

"Jordan, how did it happen that all this drama occurred in my wing, right under the nose of the smartest admin I know, and not a word found its way to my desk until recently?"

"Sir, weren't you the one who taught me one of the responsibilities of working in a command office, no matter what level of commander you are working for, is discretion? I said nothing because that was my job."

"I would have kept your confidence."

"No disrespect meant to the rank, sir, but you would have attempted to discretely interfere. The result would have been the same or worse."

"I guess I can understand that. After all, it's why I chose you for the position in the first place." Picking up some papers from his desk, signifying an end to the conversation, Colonel looked up smiling at Jordan. "All right, Jordan, get the hell out of my office. I got stuff to do."

"I am glad we have this time, sir. I have some news, and I wanted you to hear it directly from me."

Slowly putting his papers down, Colonel Wilson looked at Jordan as if really seeing him for the first time. "I'm about to lose you too, huh?"

"Yes, sir. If I can jump qualify, I'm returning to my team."

"Truthfully, Jordan, we both know you'll qualify. I think returning is a wise decision and one well overdue. You've taken a lot of flak in your barracks over this Sergeant Jackson thing. I know that asshole Lieutenant Miles fueled that fire, too. Besides, you've hidden behind that desk long enough, and I don't want to kick that candy ass lieutenant in the head if he finds out you're gay."

Stunned into silence, Jordan turned to leave the office.

"Don't worry, Jordan, I didn't ask, you didn't tell, and I never will. You just make sure you get back to your unit and continue to make us proud. I let them pull EJ out from under my nose. That will never happen again. You have any problems when you get back, I'm your first phone call. Understood?"

"Yes, sir." Jordan once again turned to exit the room.

Jordan left the wing commanders' office with a lighter heart than he'd had since the day he left EJ at base ops for the last time. He'd not heard from his friend since then. He wondered what had happened to him and what he decided to do. Whatever EJ's decision, Jordan now had made his own choice. He was going back to combat search and rescue.

CHAPTER ONE

Summer 2004

Jordan Washington sat on a bench affixed to the pier of the Sayville boat basin. He stared at the endless expanse of gray water. The slight breeze fought a fruitless battle with the oppressive 90-degree heat. Behind him, past the moored boats, stood an impressive white building. His instructions told him this was the building that held Changes Clinic and the miracle worker Dr. Dale Chenault, who was going to make him all better. From Jordan's viewpoint on the pier, the building looked like it might have been someone's mansion at one time in history.

A glare from the sunlight hitting the second floor caught his attention. He gazed with appreciation at the lone bay window and wondered what type of room existed behind it. *I bet it has one hell of a view.* He rose from the bench and proceeded down the long pier toward his destination.

As he approached the entrance, Jordan was startled by the slight, bedraggled figure staring back at him. Of course, he had seen his face in a mirror before. This, however, was the first time he had a head-to-toe reflection, and the results were disheartening. His once slender frame could only be defined as skinny. His clothing hung off his shoulders as if he were a walking clothes hanger. Even the much-needed haircut and shave he'd gotten the day prior did nothing to improve the sad image of the man now walking through the doors of Changes.

He crossed the marble floor of the lobby to the concierge.

"May I help you, sir?" inquired a tall young man, impeccably attired in a pale lavender dress shirt adorned with a paisley tie. His nametag introduced him as Glenn.

"I may be in the wrong place," Jordan began. "Is this Changes?"

Glenn smiled while consulting a screen in front of him. "Unless they changed the sign on the door this morning it is. Your name, sir?"

Before he could speak, a smiling figure emerged from the elevator.

"Jordan!" EJ called as he approached. "You were never one to keep a man waiting. My father-in-law called and told me you were due in today. You look like hell, man. Let me get a look at you."

Jordan backed up as EJ drew closer. "Back up, bro. This ain't kiss-and-make-up time. What the fuck are you doing here?"

EJ came to a halt and took a long look at Jordan. "Jordan, what on earth happened to the lean firebrand I left on Kadena Air Base? You're pale, thin, and look like you've lost a good twenty pounds."

"So, tell me how you really feel," Jordan responded. "What the hell are you doing here anyway?"

EJ moved toward Jordan slowly, his hands extended like one would approach a cornered animal. Speaking as calmly as he could, he began to explain. "Like I said, my father-in-law told me you were coming here. He didn't tell me anything else, Jordan, just that you would be here today, that you would be needing a place to stay, and that that place couldn't be with me and Dale. I figured we would pick up your stuff and I would take you to meet my friend Teddy. During that time, you would tell me what you wanted me to know."

As he spoke, Jordan relaxed his countenance. He began to

walk toward EJ slowly in steps so measured, he seemed like a lion approaching its prey. EJ must have misread the approach as Jordan settling down because he was completely unprepared for the fist that connected with the right side of his face. It came with such speed and force, it sent EJ flying backward and, fortunately, into the arms of his husband, Dale, instead of the unyielding surface of the cold, hard floor.

"You son of a bitch," screamed Jordan. "I stood by you, and you just left me to deal with the fallout. Not once did you call to see if all was okay. I never heard from your ass again. I had to hear from Chief C about your little happy ever after. I know you knew I went back to combat search and rescue. I was injured and nearly died. Did I hear from you? Hell no! Not one damn word. I arrive here to stay in some hotel because I'm told only that I can't stay with the only person I know in this God-forsaken town. What the ever-loving fuck, EJ?"

At that moment, a tall slim man stepped from his position behind EJ and approached Jordan. "That's not EJ's fault. He didn't know you were in town until he spoke to my father. Staying with us while getting treated by me could create conflict of interest issues."

The light of understanding slowly crossed Jordan's face as his eyes traveled slowly from Dale to EJ and back. "Your father? But EJ just said Chief Chennault was his father-in-law, which makes you—"

Dale smiled as he cut off Jordan's sentence. "Yes, I am Dr. Dale Chenault. EJ is my husband. Neither I nor my father have discussed your information with EJ because what he knows or doesn't know is your story to tell." Placing a gentle hand on Jordan's shoulder, Dale continued, "Why don't you come upstairs with me? We can start your orientation to the program while EJ finds an ice pack for his face."

"Seems to me he's gonna need an iceberg. That's quite the shiner," commented a laughing man, who'd suddenly appeared and approached Jordan, his hand extended. "Hi, I'm Teddy, your proposed roommate. Sorry about the hotel, but I just got back into town this morning. I'm a performer and was away for a show. By the time you and Dale are done, I should be free, and we can show you—"

"Whoa, wait a minute. Who the fuck called for the clusterfuck committee?" Jordan pushed Dale's hand off his shoulder and backed away, keeping all three men in his range of vision. "Okay, I know I have an appointment with you. Dr. Dale Ch—. Sorry, I never could pronounce your last name, but Chief C was always all right with that." He looked Teddy over from head to foot and then, shaking his head, said, "I don't know what kind of home for wayward airmen you're running, but I don't know you and I'm not some foster child that needs adopting."

Jordan then turned his attention to EJ. "You... I don't know what to make of you, man. When your situation hit the air, the shitstorm was worse than a Ryukyuan typhoon, but I stood by you. Suddenly, you were gone, Major Davis was gone, and General Barton was gone. The direct hit was all cleared, but the collateral damage had just begun. Worse yet, everyone was looking at me like I had suddenly become America's most wanted. I got injured, again, and had to return to the States, only to find Michael was dead and you were just fucking MIA." Jordan finally stopped talking and took a deep breath, concentrating intently on the patterns in the marble floor. "I was alone," he whispered.

Teddy cleared his throat his mouth, catching Jordan's attention. He opened his mouth to reply, but before he could, Dale caught his attention and signaled him to hold his peace. That accomplished, he turned again to Jordan and carefully guided him toward the elevator. "Why don't we start this over? Hi, I'm Dr. Dale Chenault. Let's go upstairs and get you sorted."

"That's a good idea," Jordan replied. "I'm gonna warn you, though, I think I'm all talked out."

Dale tilted his head to one side and smiled. "How do you stand on listening?"

"I think I can handle that."

"Good, then let's go upstairs."

With that they entered the elevator, which had just arrived, leaving a stunned EJ and Teddy behind.

CHAPTER TWO

The ride upstairs took seconds, but Jordan felt like it would never end.

"What floor are we going to?"

"Second. Why?"

"I just I don't—" Jordan's answer was interrupted when the elevator stopped, and the doors opened. He leapt from the elevator like the hounds of hell were behind him.

Dale stepped out and calmly led Jordan into his office. "Come in Jordan. Have a seat. Let's get to know one another."

"Listen, I'm a mess," Jordan said as they sat down in the comfortable chairs facing each other. "I take my meds. I've done the talking thing at Walter Reed, and most of the time, I'm okay. I don't know what set me off downstairs. It was suddenly too much, and I was unprepared for all that."

Dale listened carefully, then rose quietly to retrieve a pad from his desk. "I often find that the best place to start is at the beginning. In your case that might cover a lot of ground that you have already walked over with the psych department at Walter Reed. So how about we start with what brought you to Changes, besides my father's suggestion."

"My most recent injuries made me no longer fit for duty, even with rehab. They were just barely able to save my left leg. I was discharged with a one hundred percent service-connected disability from military service as I lay recovering in the hospital. The combination of drugs the doctors had me on for pain, inflammation, and what they claimed was PTSD made me restless. I returned home to discover Michael, my partner, had been killed in an auto accident." Fighting hard to hold back the tears threatening to form, Jordan got up and began pacing in the spacious office. The view of Great South Bay through the large window afforded him a moment of calm. Taking a few deep breaths, he continued his story. "That was the last straw for me. Michael was my true north. Without him, I was restless, rudderless, and unable to focus. My mood was up one minute and down the next, and nothing seemed to help. Desperate, I returned to DC and tried, without success, to get seen at the VA hospital. There's a waiting list for mental health treatment a mile long, so my primary doctor wrote me a script and sent me on my way. That's when I ran into your dad, and the rest you know."

Dale stood and walked over to Jordan, interrupting his pacing path. "Jordan, our program can get you started, but I think, given all you've been through, there is a better solution for getting you on your feet again." Dale pulled a sheet of paper and a business card from the top drawer of his desk. "I have a friend, a fellow counselor, who has a unique way of dealing with anxiety-driven disorders. He's had some amazingly good results with veterans with PTSD."

"So, what am I now, the neighborhood doorknob? Is everybody just gonna get a turn?"

"No, Jordan. What you are is an injured airman who needs very specific kinds of help. We have counselors and groups here, and we are very successful. What makes us the best is we also have a network of resources. The care we use for helping you get your life back is designed to be as unique as the circumstances that led you here."

Jordan sat down, reclined back in the chair and covered his eyes with his hands. *It's game time, Jordan. Either open the chute or inherit the earth.* He leaned forward to rest his forearms on his legs, looked up at Dale, cleared his throat, and asked, "Okay, so how do we make this happen?"

"Well," Dale said with a smile. "I know you like hockey. How do you feel about the Denver Avalanche?"

Jordan let out a loud laugh. "Colorado, huh? Okay. Let's do it."

"His name is Ron Cochran. He was here this week on other business and was leaving when you arrived. I'd considered asking him to stay and meet you in case my instincts were right, based on your records from Walter Reed, but decided to give us a chance to get to know each other first." Dale moved back to his desk and consulted his calendar. "It's gonna take some time to arrange your travel and accommodations. I am guessing—"

"I can drive my truck," Jordan said. "It has a tall cap on the back, and the bed is completely outfitted for me to sleep in."

"Do you know how long of a drive that is?"

"No, but I love driving and camping in my truck. She's all tuned up, has new tires, and I can shower at truck stops. Tell you what. I'll check in with you each night when I stop."

"Well, I can't stop you if you're sure. I'll contact Ron and let him know you're gonna be on your way. I do want you to check in with the VA in Cheyenne and get registered there so you can continue to get your meds without interruption. I will see if I can't get you set up with the VA Psych Clinic in Red Deer." Dale pulled a business card out of his wallet and handed it to Jordan. "Ron connected me to the psychiatrist in charge there. I'll call him and let him know you're en route. He'll be waiting to hear from you. This way you won't hit the wall you did in DC."

Jordan leapt out of his seat and headed for the door. "Okay, then, I'll be on my way."

"Hold your horses, Jordan. This is going to take time to set up.

In the meantime, we need to extend your accommodations here. I take it you've no interest in going to stay at Teddy's?"

"I'm not destitute or without resources. I'll stay at my hotel and check in with you. That way I can be on my way without the drama."

Dale opened a folder and pulled a large index card from it. "This is your treatment schedule while you're here. Since you're not staying with Teddy, that makes the way clear for you to be in his group. He's my best counselor." Dale then got up and walked back around to the front of his desk. He crossed his arms as he leaned against the smooth polished wood of the mahogany structure. He cleared his throat. "About EJ..."

"Look, congratulations to you and him. I can't be worried about EJ right now. I got my own shit to square up." Jordan took the card from Dale's outstretched hand. "Thanks, Doc. I'll see you tomorrow." He perused the card. "After group." With that, Jordan exited the office, found the stairs, and made his way to the lobby. *Colorado! I'll just be damn.* Shaking his head and chuckling, he waved goodbye to Glenn and exited Changes.

• • •

Ron Cochran leaned back in his chair on Vincent's outdoor patio, slowly sipping his iced tea. *Funny, the town keeps changing yet, Vincent's remains the same.*

Located on the edge of the small downtown area of Red Deer, Vincent's, while not an official gay bar, was known for being the popular watering hole and hang-out space for the local gay community. The outdoor patio gave a great view of his beloved Rocky Mountains. At night the lighting seemed to blend in with the stars to give off a romantic glow. In contrast and to keep the restaurant family-friendly, the center of the patio included a play area. That way parents could enjoy a cocktail with their meals while watching their young ones play. On weekend nights, live music added to the allure of the place.

He loved living in the beautiful Northern Colorado foothills. His home there was close enough to Red Deer that he could socialize with his friends whenever he chose, and yet far enough up in the foothills that everyone who knew him called first before making the trek to visit. His success at providing service animals with special talents to patients with hard-to-resolve, anxiety-driven problems was becoming renowned in multiple states. It didn't hurt that his connection network included the psychiatric specialists treating veterans with PTSD. His business, Pawz with a Cause, had proven to be so much more successful than he'd imagined when he first started out more years ago than he cared to remember. He enjoyed his work because it allowed him to live life on his terms and timetable while contributing to the health and welfare of a highly-troubled population.

His success included placing Sweetie, a lovable and calm Labrador retriever, with Troy Johnson, an Afghanistan war veteran with very resistant PTSD. As if thinking brought the man into view, Ron looked up to see his friend walking toward him. He'd met Troy when he brought Sweetie to see Dimitri, Troy's partner, to receive successful treatment for her abdominal cancer. Sweetie adopted Troy almost immediately. It was an amazing success for which Ron refused to take the credit, as it was never his intention to pair Sweetie with anyone. She had been the ambassador for his service animal business.

He smiled as the two approached him, noting that Sweetie, though happy to see him, remained dutifully at Troy's side, tail wagging a mile a minute.

"Ah, Sweetie, how are you doing, girl? You still in love and taking care of your master?"

"Well, hi, Ron," Troy said with mock indignation. "Chopped liver here. How am I doing? Oh, just fine. Yes, thank you. I'd love a glass of iced tea on this hot afternoon."

"Oh, stop with the drama, Troy. It's so unattractive." Looking around for the partner that was rarely away from Troy's side, Ron asked, "Where's Dimitri?"

"He can't make it, but he said he'll catch up with us later. What's up?"

"I have a new prospective client coming up. Dale Chenault is sending one of his vets, a young airman who's been to hell and back, to train with a service dog. You guys are close in age, and I thought a small, quiet get-together might be a nice welcome to the area."

Troy looked down at the snow-white German shepherd sitting quietly at Ron's feet.

"Sounds good. Uh, who's this?"

"This is Deejay. I found him in a shelter when I was on one of my puppy-scouting trips. He was quite the active little pup that had probably been deserted. Someone had found him but couldn't keep him. The shelter techs were overjoyed when I took him because he was gonna have to be put down if they couldn't home him." Ron reached down to scratch Deejay behind the ears. Deejay leaned into the cuddle, his tail drumming a staccato beat on the ground. "I loved his temperament, he's obviously been well cared for somewhere. His training with me has been seamless. All he needs now is to be chipped, and he'll be set for his prospective new master."

"Have you met this guy yet?"

Ron stared off into the distance as he answered. "I was still at Dale's clinic the day he arrived. He was having a real hard time. Too many people were already there to greet him and help make plans for his life. He became seriously agitated, and that was no time to add another stranger to the mix. Good looking man though. He's tall, slim, and has the most amazing eyes you ever wanted to see. They seemed to keep changing color depending on how the light hit them."

Laughing, Troy threw a paper napkin in Ron's direction. "Wipe your mouth, you horndog, you're drooling. I don't think having his bones jumped by the dog trainer is a part of his treatment plan. Anyway, how do you even know he's gay?"

"He was ranting on about being left behind and alone. All of the people he was ranting about were men. Besides, Dale's clinic specializes in helping vets suffering from the effects of Don't Ask, Don't Tell. That law left a lot of wounded men and women in its wake."

"And you want to kiss his boo-boos and make them all better," teased Troy.

"Kissing boo-boos ain't exactly my style, but I wouldn't mind... never mind."

"Give, man. Mind what?" Troy kept pushing until it became clear Ron wasn't going to bite.

Rising slowly, Ron turned to shake hands with Troy and scratch Sweetie behind the ears. "Give some thought to my idea. I don't want his arrival here to be traumatic like it was when he got to Changes, so I thought I'd give him some time to get settled in and then maybe you and Dimitri could meet us here for a beer or something." With that, Ron left the patio, and after securing Deejay in the truck, climbed in and drove off. He'd drop Deejay off at the training center and then drive over to the general store. His friend Jenny was sure to have a fresh batch of her special Krispy Treats cooling in the music room. They'd have a beer and talk about nothing, and while he was there, he would confirm the cabin he'd reserved for his new client.

CHAPTER THREE

Jordan let out a heavy sigh as he finally made the final adjustments to his stuff in the back of his 2004 Chevy Colorado. It was a beautiful vehicle, gunmetal gray with a matching high-top cap on the bed. Outfitting it so he could sleep in the back had taken a huge bite out of his savings, but it was more than worth it.

When Dr. Chenault talked to him about going to Colorado, he thought he was leaving right away. Instead, he'd had three months of counseling, groups, and medication adjustments before Dale was willing to chance him doing the trip by car. Jordan hated talking about his time in Iraq, and he really didn't want to talk about his last days there. But talk he did. *The only way over it is through it.* He was really looking forward to the journey and the alone time it would provide.

He laughed out loud as he remembered his conversation with EJ when he got his first look at the vehicle.

"Let me get this straight. You're gonna sleep in this thing while you're on the road? You do know that it's fall and the farther northwest you go, the colder it gets. How you gonna stay warm at night?"

Jordan pulled a blanket forward enough to show EJ the plug made to fit the cigarette lighter. "Dude, you can get just about any damn thing on Amazon." He then produced the Zippo hand warmers. "A couple of these in the sleeping bag with me and I am as warm as a loaf of bread in the oven."

EJ did a walk around the truck, looking it over and checking the tires.

"You want me to pop the hood so you can check the oil and belts as well?" Jordan asked, laughing at the way EJ was examining everything like a pilot conducting a flight precheck.

"Nah," EJ said, staring off into the distance. "You've never been reckless." He then walked over to Jordan and put one hand on his shoulder. "I'm glad we got our issues squared away before you left. I'm sorry I didn't check back in and make sure you were okay."

"Forgiven and forgotten, man. I had no idea of what you were going through here." Jordan looked at EJ and started laughing. "I can't believe you hid from your own parents, though. Although, now that I've met your mom, I'm beginning to wonder which one of us needs the psychiatric treatment. Your mom is scary, and you're insane for hiding anything from her."

Jordan remembered that conversation like it was yesterday. *Well, maybe that's because it was, dufus.* He began to look around. EJ and Teddy asked him not to leave without saying goodbye. *They need to get a move on. I want to be ahead of the morning traffic.* Just as the thought cleared his head, he looked up to see Teddy and EJ approaching.

Handing him a large ice cooler type container, EJ answered Jordan's puzzled look. "My mom says safe travels. Don't forget to call and check in. And don't make her hunt your ass down in Colorado." He then hugged Jordan and stepping away said, "I can't say I'm anxious to see you go, though. I mean, I get it that you need specialized help, but what's so special about a dog in Colorado? We've got service dog training academies right here in New York."

"I know," said Jordan. "But Dale says Ron Cochran has a reputation for the way he trains his dogs alongside the prospective client. The vast majority of them are trained from puppies. Those that aren't, still start out really young. Besides, PTSD is his specialty. He works in conjunction with the psychiatrists in charge of the various VA programs out west."

Jordan leaned against the lift gate of the truck, crossed his arms over his chest, and faced his friends with a look of intent determination. "There's a VA Hospital in Cheyenne. They run a specialized mental health clinic for Gulf War vets with PTSD in Red Deer. Dale spoke to a Dr. Mason, who is the program director. Dr. Mason knows Ron and has a high opinion of his program as well."

Jordan stood and put his hands on EJ's shoulders. "I need this, bro. More than I need air, I need this, and I need to do it in a place where I have room to think and mourn in peace."

"I know," EJ said, nodding in agreement. "All right, mount up and get out of here."

Turning to Teddy, Jordan extended his hand. Teddy took it and pulled him in for a hug. "Yo, man, if you need to come back this way, the room will always be ready and waiting."

"Teddy's Home for Wayward Vets and Drag Queens? I'll hold you to that on one condition. You gotta learn to dry the panty hose and costume stuff somewhere else. The ass padding on the rack in the bathtub was especially scary. Seriously though, thanks for making room for me when I got tired of hotel rooms."

"Yeah, well, in the meantime, make sure you keep this in your pocket at all times," Dale said as he walked up on the three men. He handed Jordan a card.

In case of emergency, please notify Dr. Ordell Chenault-Jackson or Elijah Chenault-Jackson @ (631) 504-4500.

On the back, he had written the address of the Red Deer clinic, Dr. Mason's number, and the address and phone number of Ron Cochran at Pawz with a Cause.

Jordan pocketed the card and climbed in the truck. As he

started it up, EJ knocked on the window and spoke through the glass, "Call and check in when you stop, okay?"

Smiling, Jordan said, "Yes, mom." And he drove off.

• • •

The trip to Colorado was beautiful and uneventful. Jordan took his time, often going off the path to enjoy the sights from the multiple look-out points he discovered. He made his promised check-in with EJ and Dale each night before he settled down to sleep.

"Why is it taking you so long to get there?" asked an anxious-sounding EJ.

"Simmer down, *mom*. I'm enjoying the drive and doing a little sightseeing. There's a lot I haven't ever seen before and stopping to smell the roses seems to be helping me stay in control. It was a suggestion Dr. C made before our last talk." Jordan turned over on his belly, closing his kindle and placing the warmers strategically in his sleeping bag. "Anyway, I'm right outside Cheyenne parked in a truck stop. I'm gonna settle down for the night and check in at the VA in the morning. Seriously, I'm tired and all tucked in, so good night, mom."

"Don't forget to call Ron and let him know your ETA. And stop calling me mom damnit. You know I'm just— What the hell was that noise? Jordan? Jordan? Answer me, dammit. Jordan!"

CHAPTER FOUR

The ICU was so quiet, you could hear the squeak of the nurse's sneakers as they walked the empty horseshoe-shaped hall. The cardiac monitor on the wall, with its multicolored display of squiggly lines and ever-changing numbers, droned on, reporting the life signs of the still, small figure in the hospital bed. Every now and then, a yellow or red light would flash, and an alarm would signal a nurse, who walked in, reset the alarm, checked the multiple lines and wires, adjusted Jordan's intravenous drip and body position, and moved on with startling efficiency. Over the last thirty minutes, the alarms seemed to go off with greater frequency. This time the ventilator joined the symphony, and for the first time, Ron Cochran jumped up and ran to the door to see if the nurse was coming. She met him as he opened the door.

"What's wrong? Why is he coughing like that? Does he need more sedation?" Ron hated hospitals and the infuriating feeling of helplessness that had become his daily grind for the past two days.

"I turned his sedation off. We're waking him up today to see if he is ready to be extubated. He's fighting the tube in his throat because he's not aware of why he feels like he's choking." The nurse, Sharon, gently put both hands on Jordan's chest. "You're okay, Jordan. As soon as you're fully awake, we are going to see if we can take that tube out. Would you like that?"

Weakly, Jordan lifted one finger as he opened his eyes to look at her.

"Ah, there you are," she said. "Good morning. If you can work with us, we can get that tube out, okay? You'll definitely be more comfortable." She continued to speak softly as she straightened out his covers and checked the security of his wrist restraints. "Your surgery went very well. Another thirty minutes and this will be all over." She then turned to look at Ron. "While we do this, I'm gonna ask you to sit in the waiting room until we're done."

"No problem. Is he going to be okay now?"

"That will be up to him and the work you and Dr. Mason do with him."

"He will need rehab, of course. Relearning to walk won't be easy," said Dr. Hines as he entered the room and crossed, his hand outstretched to shake Ron's hand. "That crazy custom work he had done to be able to use his truck as a camper saved his life. I understand, though, his friends from New York are coming to get him." Leaning his head to one side and twisting his mouth in a quirky half smile, he continued, "That's good and bad. The sound of the crash may have been enough to bring him back to square one with his PTSD. He'd be much better remaining here under Dr. Mason's care."

"If that's what he needs, we can make that happen. He was on his way here to stay anyway. With some minor adjustments, we can still make that the plan." Ron walked over to Jordan, who looked as if he'd drifted back to sleep. Just like that day in New York, he felt so drawn to Jordan. *What is it about you that calls to me? I know almost nothing about you, yet your siren's song is so strong.* He turned to leave the room. "Let me know when you're done okay, Sharon?" he asked as he walked out, closing the door behind him.

Ron walked to the atrium at the middle of the critical care pavilion. It had an amazing, oversized bay window that looked out onto the beautiful Rocky Mountains landscape. Pulling out his phone, he dialed a number he had come to know by heart.

"How is he?" asked a voice, picking up on the first ring.

"Hello to you too, EJ. What's that? How am I doing this morning? Oh, just fine, and you? No, sitting with a total stranger like a gargoyle on a church has not been stressful at all. Thanks for asking."

"Sorry, Ron. You may never know how much Dale and I appreciate you looking out for Jordan. I failed him once. I just can't believe the drama continues."

"Well, unless you were driving the truck that lost control and hit him, this one's not on you. Anyway, he's being extubated today, and then the real healing begins."

"Okay, Dale and I will be there as soon as they say he can be released."

"That's why I'm calling. We all think it will better if he stays in Colorado as planned. Jordan wanted a peaceful place to heal. Unless that's changed, that's still gonna be the plan."

"Who's gonna take care of him while his injuries heal?"

"Unless he objects, that will be me. He can still work with Deejay. Dr. Mason says he can see him one-on-one."

"Make sure you let that be that his decision. When he first got here, he blew up when he thought people were planning his life out for him."

"EJ, no offense, but you have got to stop being such a mom." Ron looked out the window, staring at the outline of the snowcapped Rocky Mountains in the distance, and spotted the reflection of the nurse coming for him. "Listen, I gotta go. I'll call and update you later."

Ron reentered the semi darkened hospital room. Jordan lay there, the head of his bed almost bolt upright. The mask on his face, with the cool mist flowing through the small holes on each side, made him look like one of those angry cartoon characters with the steam blowing from his ears.

Jordan turned his head toward Ron as he came through the door. "Who are you?" he said in a raspy voice.

"I'm Ron Cochran. We were supposed to meet under slightly friendlier circumstances." Ron approached the bedside slowly, reaching to shake Jordan's hand. "I've been in constant contact with Dale and EJ, letting them know what happened and how you're doing."

"Gee, that's nice. Want to share?" Jordan said, then broke into a coughing fit.

Ron immediately took a couple of ice chips from a cup on the nearby overbed table. "Here, suck on these and stop trying to talk. I'll tell you what I know." After Ron gave Jordan the ice chips, he gave him a pad and pencil that had been left there as well.

"Suppose I have questions or need something?"

"Shut mouth, use pencil," Ron said, enunciating each word carefully and smiling at Jordan. Then, taking a seat, he began. "Apparently you had pulled over in a truck stop to sleep. EJ says he heard a harsh sound and then you stopped talking. It turns out you were hit at the front end of your truck by a driver who claims he lost his brakes. Had you been in the driver's seat, Jesus would be telling you this story. As it happens, your camping alterations and weird sleeping position saved your life, and the injuries are to your legs only."

Jordan picked up the pencil and wrote. *Weird sleep?*

Nodding, Ron continued. "Your head was at the tailgate end of your truck instead of the front of the bed. The chair cushion thing kept the shock from damaging your head and therefore your brain. By the way, what was that thing?"

Jordan smiled. *Backrest for reading.*

"Oh. So, all that plus the insulation padding saved your ass, man."

The pencil moved furiously, Jordan chuckling as he scrawled on the pad. *Tell EJ. He laughed when he saw it.*

"He's not laughing now. He's worried sick about you."

"Such a mom," Jordan said as he shook his head. "But a good friend." The rasp in his voice seemed to be improving. "Well, please tell my mother I am on the mend, I think, and then you can be released from babysitting duties."

"Oh, I didn't consider it babysitting. Matter of fact, I stuck around today to offer you what I hope will be a favorable proposition."

Adjusting himself in the bed, Jordan cocked his head to one side. "Now I'm truly intrigued. Do you always preposition broken-down accident victims in hospitals?"

"No, you're my first." Ron rose and walked back over to the bed. "If you recall, you were headed my way soon anyway. You're going to need rehab, and if you have suitable lodgings, that doesn't have to mean you are stuck in a nursing home with a bunch of old people."

"Where am I, anyway? I'm guessing my truck doesn't count as suitable."

"Hmm," Ron started, then let out a deep breath. "You're in the Cheyenne Veterans Hospital. Your ID in your wallet made it easy for the police to have the emergency service bring you here." Okay, now for the hard part. "Your truck is totaled," he spit out quickly. "Everything that could be rescued from it is currently at my house. I was thinking that you might join your things there and that way qualify for in-home physical therapy. The rest of the time you could get to know and work with Deejay. Dr. Mason said you and he could do one-on-one sessions there until you are able to attend clinic and group sessions."

"Who is Deejay? Wait. My truck is totaled? What did I get hit by?"

"The driver had just detached the trailer from his tractor and was moving in your direction to park and sleep in the cab when he hit your truck. Hence all the repeat leg surgeries." That said, Ron slowly pulled the covers back to reveal the left leg below-the-knee amputation.

"My leg!" Jordan's attempt at a shout came out more like a hoarse squall. "Ron, what the fuck happened to my leg?"

CHAPTER FIVE

Jordan was inconsolable. "How the hell do I survive injury during hazardous military duty twice, only to lose my fucking leg relaxing in the bed of my own damn truck? What did you do? Or what didn't you do?"

Dr. Hines, the medical doctor, entered the Jordan's room just in time to hear his ranting outburst. With him was the orthopedic surgeon, Dr. Tower.

Dr. Tower stepped up to the bedside. He looked down for a moment, then turned to face Jordan. "Jordan, I'm Dr. Tower. I headed up the team that operated on your legs. As you know, the surgery on your legs after your injuries in Iraq made you able to function as a civilian, hence the service-connected disability designation. The problem is the crushing injury from the accident destroyed all the work the military did on your left leg and didn't leave us any options. We were able to repair and save your right leg, but your left, below the knee, was damaged beyond repair." As he spoke, he examined Jordan's left thigh. "You have great muscle tone in your left thigh, and we should be able to fit you with a prosthetic in no time."

Dr. Hines spoke at that point. "A lot was lost in that accident, Jordan. The driver died, and your truck was totaled. Your leg is sadly a casualty of this mess but happily, that's the end of it."

Jordan looked at Dr. Hines as if he were truly crazy. "End of it? Doc, you talk like I'm an android. All you have to do is attach a leg from spare parts and I'll be good as new. What you don't get is I don't just wish for my leg back. I want my life back. I came here to work on my PTSD and train with a service dog. To find my soul again. How the hell am I going to fit all that in with learning to hop, huh?"

• • •

Jordan was ramping up. Ron recognized it and knew he wouldn't be able stop the emotional acceleration on his own. Men and women in that state just seemed to have no fucks left. Jordan continued ranting and raving until the medication Sharon injected into his intravenous hit his bloodstream and he succumbed to a drugged sleep.

Ron watched Jordan and his doctors interact until the sedation ended the fruitless battle. There was nothing worse than feeling helpless against forces you have no control over. Ron's mind at once went to Troy and Benny. He had placed Sweetie with Troy and Poochie with Benny. Both matches were amazingly successful even before the mutual training. Troy and Benny had gone on to live amazing, productive lives with their husbands. He didn't think bringing the whole Vincent's crew up here would do any good, but there was something he could do, he thought, as he pulled out his phone.

Some hours later and after consultation with Dr. Hines and Dr. Tower, Ron walked into Jordan's room with his surprise.

"Damn, man, didn't anyone ever teach you to kno...? What in the world? Are you trying to get thrown out of here? Dogs aren't allowed in hospitals."

"Service animals are allowed everywhere. I'm glad you're in a chair. That makes the introductions easier. His name is Deejay. He's come to see if he and you like each other."

"Oh." Jordan looked down at the snow-white adult German

shepherd. "He's the most beautiful animal I have ever seen. Hello, boy."

As if he understood Jordan, Deejay walked over and sat at Jordan's right side, deftly avoiding the injured left stump.

Just at that moment, Dr. Tower walked into the room, holding a tray. "Since you're up, I thought we'd change your dressing." He stopped as he encountered the large white shepherd sitting near Jordan. "Well, hello there. Who's this?"

Ron was clearly more than pleased when Deejay, obviously already sensing the change in Jordan's demeanor, stood and placed himself between Dr. Tower and Jordan, setting his head in Jordan's lap. The smile on Jordan's face spoke volumes.

Stroking the downy fur of the beautiful shepherd, Jordan looked up and said, "This is Deejay. He's my service dog. Maybe we can do the dressing change a little later. I am really not of the mind to deal with all that right now. I'm sure the nurse can do it if you don't have time. I'm just not in a good place, and I don't want any more sedation."

Dr. Tower nodded. "I agree, more sedation isn't going to help and will only intensify the effect of your pain medicine. I'll check on you later."

Deejay looked up at Jordan and then moved to lie down on the floor near Jordan's right leg. Ron had never been prouder of any of his animals than he was at that moment.

"How did he do that?" Jordan asked. "When Dr. Tower walked in, I was struggling to stay calm. The next thing I know, I have a furry head in my lap. It was less of a struggle to pull myself together," he paused. "Still a struggle mind you, but, controllable. Maybe this could work."

"So, what do you think of my proposal, then?"

"Do you always use your dogs to get what you want?"

"Well, so far they have been my best salesmen. But this is different." Ron walked over and sat on the side of the unoccupied bed. "This is about you having more control over your life. This VA hospital is huge, but the long-term physical therapy you need is not feasible. You could start off in-home and then work out at a local therapy center with your prosthetic. It's a good plan, but it's up to you." Ron reached over and took Jordan's hand, slowly rubbing his thumb back and forth. "Everybody involved just wants you to get your life back on the track you choose."

Jordan said nothing but looked down at the hand Ron was still stroking until Ron, feeling his face warm up, sat up and released him.

"Well, um, you think about it. Deejay and I will be back tomorrow."

"He can stay," Jordan protested.

"No, he can't. He needs to be fed, and he is not toilet trained. So, walking outdoors is definitely a requirement."

"Maybe the nurses—"

"Not on your life, boy," Sharon said as she entered the room with Jordan's meds. "Neither one of you is that cute. Well, maybe Deejay is, but cute's not enough."

Jordan brought his hands to his chest. "I'm wounded."

"Drama will get you nowhere, Mr. Washington."

"And on that note," said Ron. "Deejay and I will take our leave."

Deejay began to whimper as Ron reattached his leash.

"Looks like Deejay isn't any happier about this than I am."

"Good night, Jordan. See you tomorrow," Ron said as he led Deejay out of the room.

CHAPTER SIX

Jordan woke up to the winter sun shining through his hospital window. He'd been in the hospital for six weeks, and he was champing at the bit.

In the corner of his room sat his motorized wheelchair. God bless one-hundred percent disability benefits. His temporary prosthetic lay across the arms. The sight of it was a little disappointing. He wasn't quite ready for the prosthetic, and the wait until he was able to use it would be longer—hence the motorized chair. He grabbed his crutches, worked his way into the bathroom, made quick work of his shower, and returned to the chair near his bedside. He reached into his bedside drawer pulled out his kit bag and emptied the contents on the tabletop. Dale, EJ, Teddy, and Ron had really overdone the grooming accessories. He shaved and applied aftershave even as he wondered how fruitless it was to get all spruced up for no reason. Noting the time, he stepped up his pace, pulled on the tight stump shaper, and quickly dressed in a pair of the sweats and one of the long-sleeve tees EJ and Dale sent him. He added the kit bag to the remainder of his belongings, which were packed and ready to go.

I am so ready to go, but where? I can't say home because I don't yet have a home. Fuck, even my truck is gone. I don't know if going to Ron's house is the best idea, but what else am I going to do? If I don't get out of this hospital, I am going to lose my ever-living mind. Until I finish my rehab and my training with Deejay, I guess Ron's is the best place for me.

Jordan was so engrossed in his thoughts, he didn't realize he had company until there was a furry white head in his lap.

"Deejay! How'd you get in here, boy? Where's Ron?"

"Right here. I got all your paperwork. So, let's get your hot rod and break camp."

Jordan took a good look at his new roommate. He was dressed in what seemed to be his preferred jeans, hiking boots, and a green T-shirt. His dark hair was cut in a close military-style, and he had piercing gray eyes set deep in his tanned and weather-beaten face. Tall and broad-shouldered with an athlete's build, he was often taken to be in his mid-thirties. In another place at another time and under better circumstances Jordan couldn't help but think he'd be all over the walking wet dream.

Right behind Ron came Michael, his favorite orderly pushing a wheelchair.

"Hey Jordan!" said Michael. "I'm here to escort you on your last ride through these hallowed halls. By the way, nurse Sharon said to remind you the no speeding rule is still in effect."

Jordan moved into his scooter, got settled and then reached over to shake Michaels hand. Thanks man, you were amazing to me. I'll never forget you. "

"No worries man. I'm glad you're having such a good outcome."

Ron, hands full of Jordan's bags and belonging spoke up, "Okay ladies enough vows of undying devotion. It's time to roll out." That said he lead the small procession past the staff who'd all lined up to wish Jordan well on his way out of the unit and down the hall to the elevator bank.

When they got to the hospital entrance, the orderly remained with Jordan while Ron took Deejay and his bags and went to get the car. Jordan suddenly had a thought he'd not considered in all his time in the hospital. How are we going to fit this little minibus into anything? He was grateful for all the help the VA has provided, but he didn't even know what Ron drove.

A cherry red 2005 Chevy Colorado entered the pick-up/drop off area. *Now that's a vehicle I could use. Me, Deejay, and the bus would all fit comfortably in that beauty.* As Jordan sat salivating over the beautiful vehicle, a very familiar canine face appeared in the window.

"Deejay!" he cried out. Jordan watched in amazement as Ron hopped out of the truck cab.

"You know, if you keep your mouth open like that, flies will take residence."

"What the—? How? Who?"

"Hmmm. It's a truck, retrofitted to carry your hot rod. I think it was done by securing the platform to the bed of the truck, and as for who, all I can say is, not me. I'd have to love you to spend that kind of scratch. So before you ask me any more questions, let's get your chair on the lift and you in the cab."

Reaching into the bed, Ron started a motorized platform-looking thing rising from the truck bed and lowering to the ground. Once it was on the ground, Ron unfolded it and walked over to Jordan.

Jordan maneuvered the chair onto the lift. Then, accepting his crutches from the orderly, moved over to the cab, where he found a grab bar to assist his ingress and egress. He took a quick look and noted a matching set of bars on the driver's side. Deejay greeted him with snuggles and kisses, and then, as if on silent command, settled down in the back seat, content with his view from the window.

Ron hopped into the driver's seat and put one hand lightly on Jordan's left thigh. "I know you have a ton of questions. Let's get to my house, get you settled, and then we can talk forever."

Jordan, completely overwhelmed, nodded once, leaned back on the headrest, and closed his eyes.

The drive took about an hour, but it only felt like moments

before Jordan heard Ron say, "We're here."

Jordan looked in awe at the rustic two-story hi-ranch nestled into the foothills, with no other house in his immediate sight. As they pulled up to the garage, the door opened, revealing what Jordan could only describe as a cavernous space holding a lone white van with the words Pawz with a Cause adorned the sides.

"Your van reminds me of *Blue's Clues* with the big blue paw prints."

Laughing as he walked over to Jordan's side of the truck, Ron said, "Well, I promise I'm not Steve, but I'll say it. You've found a clue!" He continued laughing at his own bad joke. "Okay, let's get you out of the truck and see how you like the rest of the place."

Using the grab bars and his crutches, Jordan tried to maneuver his way out of the truck. He misjudged the logistics, and the next thing he knew, a pair of strong arms was holding him and lowering him to the ground. *Oh my God! This man is solid, and he smells like heaven.* It was all Jordan could do to hold back the groan as he slid past the bulge in Ron's tight-as-hell jeans. The friction was simultaneously excruciating and delicious. *Lucky for me, I'm wearing sweatpants.*

Ron moved to the back of the truck and activated the motorized platform lowering Jordan's scooter chair to the floor. Once it was on the ground he called to Jordan, "Okay, your chair is down. Hop in but remember the speed limit indoors is five miles per hour or less."

Jordan was about to ask how he was supposed to get inside when he noticed a brand-new ramp leading up to the front door. He started to head for it when Ron stopped him.

"We have a direct connection. Follow Deejay."

As if on cue, Deejay let out a bark and led Jordan through a door from the garage into the darkened house.

"Hey, where are the lights? I don't want to bump into anything."

Suddenly the room was awash in light and shouts of "Surprise!

Welcome Home!" There stood EJ, Dale, EJ's parents, Chief and Mrs. Jackson, and Chief and Mrs. Chenault, Dale's parents..

Jordan shook for a minute, but Deejay was at his side, his head in his lap, grounding him.

"Welcome home, son."

"How'd you like the truck?"

"How do you feel?"

"Okay, everybody," Dale called, gaining control of the room. "Let's back up and give the man some breathing room."

Ron took that moment to interject, "If everybody waits until you see Deejay move out of his lap and not all approach at once, he'll be fine."

Jordan could barely pay attention to what was going on, but he also didn't feel out of control or trapped in the chair like he did when the nurses all wanted to celebrate his first day mobile. He took a deep breath, allowing Deejay's presence to ground him the way he had practiced with Ron while in the hospital. "Hi, everybody. When did you all get here?"

Dale spoke first. "We put our heads together from the moment of your accident, figuring out how we could best help with your immediate needs."

EJ walked over to Jordan's chair and knelt so they were eye to eye. "I told you I wouldn't fail to have your back. My dad and father-in-law brought together what my mom calls the Chief's Council. They made sure there were no snags in your paperwork for your chair."

"Jordan," Chief Jackson said. "The man who was supposed to arrange for the shipment of EJ's bike has a friend who arranged for the truck and the lift. Once your insurance settles with you on your totaled truck, you should have most of the money for the new truck. The payments are actually better than what you were paying. We all got together to help Ron build the ramp. Dale and EJ drove the truck here."

Jordan was overwhelmed. "I just don't know how to take all this."

"You're family man," EJ said. "We take care of our own. We wanted to be here to celebrate your discharge from the hospital. Unfortunately, we're going to have to leave tonight to catch our plane back home before Manny learns too many bad habits from his uncle Teddy."

"As homecomings go, this one is top shelf. Thanks, everybody. I honestly don't know what else to say."

"I do," said Ron. "Let's eat. I'm starving, and it looks like the ladies have prepared a spread fit for a king."

CHAPTER SEVEN

The day had been hard to get through, but Deejay never left his side. Ron had appeared as if out of nowhere, discretely gave him his meds, and with Dale's help, kept the mothers from, well, mothering him to death.

Eventually it was time for everyone to leave if they were going to catch their shuttle to the airport and make their plane on time. The hugs and kisses and instructions went on forever. Finally, EJ's father Edward Jackson came to the rescue.

"Okay, ladies, let's go. EJ, Dale, it's time to roll out." Dale guided EJ through the front door with a last promise to stay in touch and be there for Jordan if he needed anything."

Ron closed and locked the doors. "Alone at last. I'd give you the ten-dollar tour, but you've got to be worn out by now. I got a ton of movies, and frankly, you've been in that chair a bit long. How about you transfer to the couch? We can relax by watching a movie."

Jordan was shaking but gave a slow affirmative nod.

"You get settled, and I'll let Deejay out to take care of his evening business. There are blankets in that basket at the end of the couch if you're chilly."

"We gonna snuggle up while we watch movies, Ron?"

A strange look passed across Ron's face, but it faded just as quickly. He turned, and whistling for Deejay, headed for the back door to let him out. Jordan had seen that look before during those last weeks in the hospital and especially during the sessions with physical therapy.

What the hell is up with that?

When Ron came back in with Deejay, he brought two bottles of beer, two bottles of soda, and a bowl of potato chips. Deejay settled on the floor below Jordan.

Taking a seat on the couch with Jordan, Ron placed the bottles and bowl on the coffee table in front of them. "I know you're taking meds, and I didn't know if you'd want beer. I noticed you'd stuck to Coke while the crowd was here, so if you want something else, we probably have it in the fridge."

Not for the first time since the accident, Jordan felt as wound up, angry, and out of focus as he had the day, he walked into Dale's clinic for the first time. "You know, this is nice, but I don't need fucking pity. I'm not some dainty little candy ass that has to be tucked in blankets or wrapped in cotton wool." Jordan knew he was ramping up, but he couldn't seem to stop the crazy man from using his mouth. "I've been severely injured in live-fire situations and survived all on my own, twice! Compared to that shit, a car accident is nothing. So tell me how much I owe you for the dog and we're fucking out of here."

Ron drew back as if he'd been slapped. "What the hell are you talking about? Jordan, you're not going anywhere at this time of night. You're overtired, man. Settle down."

Deejay kept nudging Jordan, trying to put his head in Jordan's lap, to no avail. Jordan was really out of control.

"Fine, keep the damn dog. Give me my car keys and I'm on my way."

Ron stood and calmly walked to the hook in the kitchen where he had hung the keys to the truck. "I tell you what," he said, swinging the keys on one finger, without raising his voice. "You load up your chair into the truck bed, pack in all you stuff, and get into the truck unassisted, and I'll not only give you the keys, I'll give you fool-proof directions out of here."

Sitting down on the couch near Jordan, Ron turned to face him. "If you don't manage all that shit, especially after your one extra-long day out of the hospital, you take your meds and get yourself a good night's sleep to calm down. In the morning after breakfast, we'll start over, beginning with a talk about what all is really bothering you."

"I'm not fucking helpless. That's the problem—you all think I'm helpless, but I can take care of myself. I been doing it since I was fourteen years old."

"No, Jordan. I don't think you're helpless. Neither do your friends. I do think you're tired, probably in pain, and sick of being sick. I get it, and I'll do anything to help you, except fight with you."

"You think I've got no reason to be mad? 'Cause I'm telling you, I've had it up to here with all this shit." Jordan brought his hand up to the top of his head, demonstrating his point.

Ron got up, collected the untouched beer and bottles, and returned them to the refrigerator. He came back in the room carrying Jordan's meds and a glass of water. He offered both to Jordan. "Okay, it sounds like you feel like your drowning. So how about tonight you let me, and Deejay pull you to shore, and tomorrow we can start swim lessons."

Jordan didn't even notice that he was stroking DeeJay's fur. He let out a huge sigh. "I'm not gonna win this with you, man. Give me my meds. I'll take 'em and go to bed." Anything, he thought, anything to get out of this room before I start crying.

"I'll give them to you tonight. Tomorrow, job one is organizing your stuff so you can get to it when you need to."

With that, Ron gave Jordan his medications and they both

turned in for the night.

Jordan lay in bed. He was exhausted, so why couldn't he sleep? The bedroom was large enough for the queen-sized bed and double dresser it held. The furniture was beautiful—walnut brown, sturdy, masculine. The L-shaped corner desk sported a bookshelf hutch on one side and plenty of room for a computer on the other and matched the bed and dresser.

As Jordan reran the events of the night in his head, he couldn't begin to figure out why he was so edgy, especially with Ron, the man he had spent his entire hospitalization dreaming about and lusting after.

Ron, what I wouldn't give to have one hot night with you. Yeah, right, Jordan, because successful men with their lives in order are just trolling the streets looking for the spoils of war and damaged goods. I got a truck I still don't know if I can afford or operate, a dog who at this moment is smarter than I am, and a powered wheelchair.

"Sex on wheels, fellas—get it while it's hot," Jordan said as the tears rolled down his face.

CHAPTER EIGHT

Jordan awoke to a quiet house. It had already been over a month since he moved into Ron's house. He had become accustomed to the stealthy way Ron moved from room to room and had even begun to tease him about his ninja-like gait. Jordan groaned as he stretched and considered the day. It was Saturday, which meant he could actually sleep in if he so desired. Of course, he never did, but it was a nice thought. Despite his initial doubts, the therapy sessions were working, even if they were often brutal.

The physical therapist, Douglas, put him through his paces like he was trying to qualify for the rigors of a Marine Corps drill. Jordan smiled as he thought of their sessions.

"Move it, Airman. My ninety-year-old granny does better than that. When I'm done with you, you won't be able to tell which leg is real and which is the prosthetic," he promised,

Doug kept telling Jordan how lucky he was to have the below knee amputation, which he kept calling a "BKA."

"You gonna be able to outrun that vampire dog of yours."

"Hey, don't be dissing Deejay. He'll take your bulldog ass down," Jordan protested.

Thing was that Douglas was right. Jordan *was* getting stronger every day. He spent ever-increasing time in the temporary prosthetic. Initially he was discouraged because his healing had seemed to slow down, but after what Dr. Tower called some "mop up" surgery, he was on a roll and moving like a champ.

His work with Dr. Mason and the Soldier-to-Soul Mates group was just as brutal.

Dr. Mason had started out gentle at first as he peeled back the layers of the destructive events in Jordan's life. They walked through the personal side of his military career almost one day at a time. In the beginning Jordan didn't understand what the hell all that had to do with his PTSD, but he couldn't argue with the results. If he could just bring himself to talk about Michael and his last injury in the line of duty... They remained off-limits topics. He wasn't ready.

The group was another story. It was all men, similar to the group he'd worked with in Sayville. Those brothers would call bullshit in a New York minute. One guy, Bishop, was always on his ass. They'd become close and were talking about getting together one day and seeing what that truck of his could really do. Bishop reminded him of Richard and Ron. He never let Jordan get away with a thing and called him on his stuff every time.

The best part of his healing and therapy was laying on the floor waiting for him to be ready to start the day. He and Deejay had some rocky moments at first. Jordan had to unlearn everything he thought he knew about dogs. Yes, he was the master, but Deejay was more than a pet. The socialization drills were the worst. Everyone was attracted to Deejay because of his coloring. A snow-white German shepherd was an uncommon sight. He was also less bulky than the more common black-and-brown or gray dogs in his breed. Like his master, though, his size was deceptive because Deejay was strong and fierce.

"We make quite the team, don't we, boy?" Jordan asked as Deejay rose in response to the sounds of Jordan moving around. He barked as Jordan sat up in bed moving to get settled in his chair before he noticed the crutches leaning against the nightstand.

"Oh yeah," he said. "I'm supposed to minimize time in the chair to keep my right leg strong. You could let me get away with it sometimes, though."

Jordan made quick work of getting cleaned up so he could head to the kitchen to let Deejay out for the morning. He pulled open the door and stepped smack into a human brick wall. Two arms shot out and stopped him from falling as his crutches hit the floor.

"Woah, Mario. Speed limit on crutches is sixty paces per minute," Ron said as he released Jordan long enough to retrieve the fallen crutches.

Jordan settled on his crutches. "You forget, I'm military. Normal cadence is one hundred twenty steps per minute."

"Right, sixty steps each foot. Since you only have one leg at the moment..."

"Oh, you got jokes now, huh? I think you better stick to your day job." Noticing that Deejay seemed a little restless, Jordan moved into the hallway. "Deejay doesn't seem to be enjoying the jokes either. Besides, I think he has a little business of his own to attend to."

"I'll handle that. You go get dressed. I'm starving, and I've been waiting for you to wake up."

Jordan couldn't hold it back. "You do know I can cook unsupervised. Don't worry, Ronnie. I'll protect you from the big bad stove."

"That may be, but not where we're going. No questions," he said in response to the look on Jordan's face. "Git. It's already noon and we're burning daylight"

"Settle down, sheriff. I'm a gittin'. I'm a gittin'." Continuing to laugh, Jordan moved back into his room to get appropriately dressed.

An hour and a half later they were exiting Highway 287 and pulling into the parking lot of the

Wagon Wheel Diner. Jordan stared, wide-eyed in disbelief. The entrance to the diner was constructed to look like a covered wagon. As they passed through, a sign directed all cowboys to clean the soles of their boots or remove them. An arrow pointed down to a boot scraper that looked like it was at least two hundred years old. Next to it was a shelf that held two pair of well-worn cowboy boots.

"Did we go through some kind of time warp?" Jordan asked. "Is someone really walking around in there in their stinky stocking feet?"

"It gets better," Ron said. Smiling as they were met by a hostess and were led inside, he pointed out the room made to look like a forest. In the center was a campsite where six kids sat cross-legged on the ground around a very realistic-looking cook fire and eating beans and hotdogs out of tin plates.

Jordan's eyes lit up. "That's pretty cool, but I've had my fill of eating cross-legged on the ground."

Laughing, the hostess explained, "That's our party room. Even if you wanted to use it, the room's pretty much booked up for the next few months. After the first couple of parties, word spread like wildfire. Now we have a long waiting list, and people are already booking for next year." She showed them to a cozy booth in the corner by the front window. "This is your table."

One of the kids attending the party and broke loose from the group. "Oooh, what a pretty doggie. Can he come play with us? It's my birthday and it would be fun and—"

"No, Leslie," called a frantic-sounding female. She looked from Deejay, who sat amazingly still, to Jordan. "I'm sorry. I left for one moment to help my daughter clean up. He is a beautiful dog, though."

Jordan turned to the little boy. Leslie? "His name is Deejay. You see this yellow vest he is wearing and all the tags on his harness?" Seeing Leslie nod a quick yes, Jordan continued, "That means he is working and not here to play."

"What's his job, mister?"

"My name is Jordan, and Deejay here stays by me so I can be outside without feeling bad."

"Oh. Maybe my mommy can get a work dog for Sarah."

Jordan looked to the mother for clarification.

"My daughter Sarah has seizures after receiving a traumatic brain injury. She got hurt twice because she doesn't get enough of an aura to warn her or she doesn't recognize them and can't make herself safe."

Ron took a card from his pocket and handed it to the mother. "I train service dogs and actually have a traumatic brain injury client who has had great success with his dog, Poochie. I'm sure he'll be more than happy to talk to your daughter and answer any questions she may have on a first-hand-experience level."

"Did you train DeeJay?"

"He did," Jordan said. "As you can see, his training is impeccable."

"Well, if Poochie is as great an ambassador as Deejay here, I think we can definitely do business. Thank you," she said, looking at the card and grabbing her son by the hand. "We better get back to the party. I will call you next week."

• • •

Jordan and Ron resettled in their seats in the cozy oak booth. Menus were already at their places, along with water, a tin coffee pot, and silverware wrapped in linen napkins dyed to look like burlap. They ordered their meals. Service was amazingly fast, and before they knew it both, men were tucking into immense steaming, hot plates of steak, eggs, home-fried potatoes, and Texas toast slathered with butter.

Ron reached out to pour them each more coffee. "You know, we always say we met at the hospital. That's true, but I've seen you before. I was there the day you arrived at Chances." He stopped a moment. A strange expression quickly passed over his face, and then he asked, "You mind if I ask you a question?"

Choking back a laugh, Jordan responded, "That hasn't stopped you before. Go ahead."

Ron straightened his posture, put down his coffee cup, and wrapped his hands around it. As he looked up, Jordan couldn't help but feel mesmerized by the intensity in those eyes staring at him as if they could see through him.

"Who is Michael?" Ron's voice was whisper quiet.

Of all the questions, damn. Jordan swallowed hard. "Why do you ask? I mean, how do you even know? I never told anybody—"

"Whoa there, Sundance. Remember, I said I was at Chances when you came in. Well, I was there as the whole crowd converged on you at once and you had that cataclysmic meltdown. During all that madness, you made a statement about Michael being gone, and I just wondered why that had such an effect on you compared to all the others you listed. If you remember, you were wound pretty tight. But when you mentioned Michael, you looked more distraught than agitated."

Jordan nodded in acknowledgement. *I can't seem to tell Dr. Mason, but Ron has been the person I've trusted to catch me when I fall—literally. Maybe it's time I took the chance with telling someone.* He let out a deep sigh. "I'll make you a deal. I'll tell you mine if you tell me yours."

Drawing his head back and pointing to himself, Ron retorted, "Mine? What do you mean, mine?"

"Well, you run a business that would be successful anywhere. I dare say you would probably have much more business in a more urban area, like Denver. Yet here you are, situated in the foothills of the Rocky Mountains." Jordan took a sip of his cooling coffee, then topped off his and Ron's cups. "I ain't criticizing. I'm just saying I know there's a story there. So I'll tell you mine if you tell me yours. Deal?" He extended his hand.

It took Ron a few moments to respond, and just as he thought

Ron was going to balk at the deal, he stuck his hand out. "Deal. You first, but how about we go somewhere we can talk uninterrupted by the well-meaning waitress who really needs this table to empty out and gain new paying customers?"

"We're paying customers!"

"True, but we've had our service. She needs a new set of folks so she can increase her income. Know what I mean?"

Jordan loved the way Ron ran that phrase together like it was all one word. It never failed to make him laugh. They left the diner and made their way back to the truck. He got Deejay secured in the back seat, settled himself on the passenger side, and after Ron started the truck, they drove off.

An hour later they were back at the house. Ron started a fire in the family room fireplace while Jordan went to change into the soft sweatpants that made lounging easier. The day had flown by, with breakfast being more like a late brunch. The sky outside his window was already showing signs of the approaching early evening. As his thoughts turned to Ron setting up the family room, Jordan wondered what it would be like for this to be the beginning of a more enjoyable evening, lying together watching movies or listening to music. *Stop dreaming, Jordan. You're here to recuperate and rehabilitate, nothing more. This isn't a romance novel. Get a grip.* With that thought, Jordan got himself into his chair and moved into the family room. When he got there, he found Ron had laid out some cheese and crackers and a bottle of wine. *How romantic. Oooh yeah, this is gonna help me stay realistic big-time.*

"Wow! This looks cozy." Jordan transferred to the couch and got settled. He looked to his left just in time to see that expression on Ron's face once again. *I'm gonna find out what that look means if it kills us both.*

"I thought you might like a glass of wine and a slight nosh even though we had that big meal at the diner." Ron stirred the fire and added another log. "I know I'm not going to eat a regular meal again." He stood, dusting off his jeans as he rose. "How about you?"

"Nah, I'm good."

Ron moved to the couch beside Jordan. "Okay, then. We have food, fire, and firewater." He turned to look at Jordan. "Michael?"

"I don't know where to begin," Jordan said, looking down at his hands in his lap.

Gently placing two fingers under his chin, Ron raised Jordan's face. "I always find that starting at the beginning works well."

Jordan picked up both wine glasses and handed one to Ron. Clinking his glass to Ron's he said, "Here's to the beginning." With that they both drank deeply from their glasses and Jordan began his story.

CHAPTER NINE

"Michael and I would have been together for twenty years next March We met in 1988 when I was on a visit to the historic Freedom Trail in Boston and came upon a sight that stopped me cold. There was this handsome male photographer sitting cross-legged in the grass." Jordan leaned back against the soft couch back and closed his eyes. "One of the first things I ever notice about a person is their eyes. Michael's eyes were a golden brown so soft, they reminded me of caramel. They were as penetrating as they were warm." Smiling at the memory, Jordan continued, "When those eyes were trained on me, I swore Michael could see clear down to my soul.

"We talked and walked and got to know each other over lunch. I was leaving soon for basic training and was getting in some limp, lame, and lazy time before I had to report to the induction center. We stayed in touch by mail. Michael signed his letters *Michèle*. We were always careful not to get me busted, but the name change came as a surprise when I got his first letter." Jordan sat up and looked at Ron with a wry grin. "I told everyone *she*," he said, making air quotes, "was French.

"In 1990, after basic and the never-ending technical training schools, I was stationed at Hanscom Air Force Base outside of Boston as a personnel specialist. We decided fate was on our side and the relationship continued to grow. When Michael posed as a cousin who could well afford to shoulder the rent, I gained permission to reside off base and we moved in together."

That revelation made Ron sit up so fast, he almost knocked over his wine. "Considering the military position on homosexuality, you guys were seriously playing with fire."

"Yeah, and as long as I was stateside, we pulled that act. It became easier when I was promoted to an NCO, but not by much." Jordan shifted in his seat and began massaging his stump.

"Is it aching?" Ron asked, reaching into the coffee table drawer for the bottle of massage oil he kept there. Jordan considered, for a moment, questioning the presence of the massage oil, thought better and simply nodded. Ron rolled up the leg of the sweatpants and began to methodically massage the stump.

Sighing in pleased contentment, Jordan continued, "I applied for jump school, and in 1995, as an enlisted para-j, I was assigned to the combat search and rescue unit attached to the tactical fighter wing first at Davis-Monthan Air Force Base in Arizona, and then one year later, I was moved to Kadena Air Base, Okinawa. Michael couldn't follow me to Okinawa, and that was probably the beginning of the problems between us. I was shot while performing a rescue attempt during the Gulf War, and Michael wasn't notified until I was in a position to get a letter mailed out to him. That meant quite a few of his letters went unanswered or were sometimes misdirected, causing them to be returned to sender—unopened, thank God. To say he was not pleased was a gross understatement."

Deejay began to whine, and Ron got up to let him out. When he returned, he refreshed both of their glasses.

Jordan took a long drink as he approached the more painful part of his story. "I wrote long letters to Michael, who was still smarting from the way he had been notified of my first injury by a friend on leave. He said he didn't like Richard, that Richard gave off a vibe like there was more between us than friendship. This is not a quote, but Richard said something like 'I am his personal go-between, so contact me for anything you need to know.' Michael burned the info in the sink.

"Michael was beginning to tire of his solitary existence. Military wives had support groups. All Michael had was an understanding brother and hateful parents who blamed me for Michael straying away from the 'ways of the righteous.'

"In September 2001, just after I sent Michael a long letter promising to apply for an instructor position in the United States, where we could again live together, the Twin Towers were attacked. My combat search and rescue unit was immediately deployed to support Operation Iraqi Freedom. This is where, during a rescue, I became injured to the point I was no longer fit for duty, even with rehabilitation. That's when I was designated disabled, awarded the purple heart for being injured under fire, and retired from military service, all as I lay recovering in Walter Reed Hospital in Washington, DC.

Jordan drained the contents of his glass as he continued his story.

"The only thing I wanted was to get home to Michael and fix whatever pain caused him to stop writing me or answer my calls to let him know I was on my way home for good. I purchased a ring on my way home. I was going to propose. When I got to our apartment, I found everything that belonged to Michael and some things that were mine gone from the apartment." Jordan's eyes began to burn as the tears slowly ran down his face.

Ron rose and got napkins from the kitchen and handed them to Jordan. As he moved back toward his seat on the couch, he picked up the bottle and poured them each another glass of wine. He handed one to Jordan and then sat back down on with his glass in his hand. Jordan didn't bother to wipe the tears. He let them roll down his face as he took a drink from his glass and then continued his story.

"I had never been on good terms with Michael's parents.

They were fundamental Christians who blamed me for Michael professing to be gay and in love. They refused to tell me anything about Michael's whereabouts, saying Michael was forever out of my reach.

"Michael's brother David, on the other hand, was another story. Michael had come out to him shortly after his sixteenth birthday. I called David, who sadly informed me Michael had been killed in a robbery gone wrong as he was making his way home one night. As it happens, Michael died on the same day I was injured in the failed rescue. It had been six months before I was able to come home, what with surgeries, rehabilitation, and administrative actions. I just thought the unanswered letters and unreturned phone calls were Michael's way of letting me know he had reached the end of his rope."

At this point Jordan's tears were flowing like a waterfall, and he made no attempt to stem the ever-increasing tide. Ron, put down his glass and pulled Jordan into his arms and held him as the cathartic tears fell. After a few minutes, Jordan took a deep breath, a large sip of his wine, and continued.

"David didn't contact the Red Cross because he knew outing me would cause me to receive a dishonorable discharge even after all my years of service. When his parents stripped the apartment of all of Jordan's belongings, David went in with them and managed to rescue the things he knew I would consider precious, like photo albums and saved letters, especially the ones that Michael had refused to open or, because of the accident, had never received. The answering machine, full to capacity with messages from me, sat alone on the counter in the kitchen. David had discreetly pulled out the tape and slipped it into his pocket. He gave it to me with everything else. I used to play it over and over just to hear Michael's voice on the greeting."

Ron continued to comfort Jordan, who laid his head on his shoulder as he sobbed unrestrained. "Shhh, babe. I've got you." Ron ever so slowly began to kiss the tears on Jordan's face.

Jordan was tired and wrung out but telling his story also made him feel some measure of relief. Ron was the only person to ask honestly about something other than his injuries, the battles, or his childhood. He was also the very first person Jordan had trusted with this story, and it felt good. Not as good as the soft kisses caressing his face, but good all the same. Jordan couldn't remember when he'd last felt this way, and since Ron wasn't moving him back to his original place on the couch, maybe it was okay if he chose to simply stay there in Ron's arms and just be.

CHAPTER TEN

Ron continued to hold Jordan as the tears gave way to soft sobs and then the even breathing of sleep. He softly stroked his back and shoulders until there was a peace about Jordan's face Ron had not seen before. Despite the medications and therapy, Jordan continued to suffer nightmares. Ron could hear him shouting in the still mountain nights. He never wanted to talk about the dreams the next morning, and Ron didn't push. He thought back to the gut-wrenching crying and wondered, not for the first time, how much losing Michael weighed on the heavy-laden heart of this man who had given so much in the name of duty.

He looked down at Deejay laying on the floor in front of the waning fire. "What do you think, boy? Should we put him to bed?" *I should probably put him in bed where he'd be more comfortable, but he fits so well in my arms and it feels so good to finally hold him. Ah, well, Ron, let's not be selfish. The man needs a good night's sleep.* Carefully he cradled his precious bundle in his arms and made the trek down the hall, with Deejay faithfully following behind. How he managed to get Jordan in the bed, out of his sweats, and under the covers without waking him, Ron would never know. Deejay settled on his blanket and lay down, seemingly content that his master was peaceful.

Ron returned to the family room just in time to hear his phone ringing.

"Dale, please don't tell me you have another client so soon."

"You really need to take some of your money and invest in lessons in the social graces. How is Jordan? If EJ didn't have such a demanding job, I'd have to put him in restraints to keep him in New York."

"Oooooh, kinky. When did you two add that level of fun to your relationship?"

"Comedy is just not your strong suit," Dale said dryly. "Seriously, how is Jordan? I spoke to Dr. Mason, and he said he felt Jordan was seriously holding back on the core causes of his rage, and quite frankly, he's certain that Michael's death is at the heart of it."

"You may be right, but I'm not comfortable sharing what he's told me in confidence."

"Now, Ron, you—"

"Don't pull that on me, Dale. Aren't you the man who helped EJ hide from his own mother and father for a month? Furthermore, I can assure you he has no plan to commit acts dangerous to himself or others. Lastly, I am not his therapist, so again I have no professional obligation. You and Dr. Mason are just gonna have to work it out and wait it out."

"Okay, okay, down, boy. I'm not trying to violate the man's privacy rights. If I sound that way, I apologize."

Ron ran his hand through his hair and then picked up his wine glass to drain the last of the liquid left in it. "It's okay, man. I just feel very protective of him, and he's really had a lot on his emotional plate. If I can help it, he won't ever have to deal with so much again."

"Hmmm. Listen, my friend. This sounds like much more than friendship. What you do is your business, but you can't wrap him in cotton batting to save him from himself. From what I've learned of Jordan, he'll never stand for it either."

"Oh yeah, he is quite independent. He and Deejay are more than bonded. I'm not looking forward to the day he decides to move on."

"Then let him know that, airhead! If your intentions are what I think they are, then you need to show him you not only see him as a man but want and desire him because of it."

There was a long silence on the other end of the line. It was so long that Ron thought maybe the connection was lost. Just as he was about to call out to see if anyone was there, the soft but firm baritone of EJ came through the line.

"Ron, this is EJ. I could tell when I was there you were attracted to Jordan. Fact is, I could also tell he's attracted to you. Seriously, what's not to like in either one of you? Thing is, and this is a warning, don't play him close or hurt him in any way. If you do and he doesn't kill you, I will."

The chill in EJ's voice gave Ron a moment's pause.

"Yeah, okay, EJ. I'll keep that in mind."

In the background, Ron heard Dale speaking. "Give me that phone, crazy man, and stop being such a mom." Then Dale had the phone again. "Ron, don't mind EJ. He gets better as Manny gets older."

"Yeah, kids will do that for you." Ron let out a long yawn. "Listen, it's been a long day and I'm taking Jordan to the Mosh tomorrow. They are having a cool jazz concert."

"The Mosh? What's a Mosh?"

Ron laughed. "Oh my God, Dale. How soon you forget. Moshwhalla, where we have all the concerts when the weather turns acceptable."

"Oh yeah. Gotta bring EJ up there to experience that. Y'all gonna go by the general store for some of Penny's special Krispy Treats before the show?"

"Do you know you giggle like a girl? To answer your question, maybe. Now I gotta split. It's been a long day and I'm tired."

They said their good nights, and Ron made quick work of cleaning up the family room and extinguishing the fire. He was looking forward to tomorrow night. He'd made the reservation to include a table for dinner on the Poudre River. His friend was one of the owners, and they'd make sure Ron and Jordan had a prime spot from which to not only enjoy dinner, but the show also.

Yeah I know it's a bit romantic, but like Dale said, I gotta show him I see him as a man, not a client or a rescue project. Hopefully tomorrow will be a good start.

With that thought, Ron locked up and started down the hall to turn in for the night. He stopped outside Jordan's bedroom door. "Sleep well," he whispered. "Here's praying your nightmares take the night off."

CHAPTER ELEVEN

"Where are we going?" Jordan asked for what had to be the one thousandth time. "I know you said it's a surprise, but I don't like surprises."

"You'll like this one," Ron said as he turned the truck into a gravel parking lot.

Jordan had a hard time taking his eyes off the rustic sign with the life-sized buffalo statue beneath it. It looked like paper mâché, with dried leaves for its mane. American flags were stuck in the ground along the planter box that had probably seen better days. Jordan expected cowboys to come up and hitch their horses to the fence post at any moment.

"Were just making a short stop. I want you to meet my friend Penny," Ron said as he opened Jordan's door. "We will only be a moment, so we can leave Deejay in the truck."

Jordan climbed down carefully, using the grab bars for support the way Douglas had taught him. This was his first full-on outing with his new permanent prosthetic. He was more than excited when Douglas stopped by that morning to give it to him. He'd said when it arrived in the morning's delivery, he just had to reward all of Jordan's hard work by not making him wait until Monday's therapy session. Over his protests, Ron had still put his crutches in the back seat with Deejay, "just in case."

They went inside, and Jordan thought he had stepped into *The Twilight Zone*. Every square inch of surface in the store was covered with novelties, antiques, jewelry, clothing, and accessories of every kind. Hanging on the wall was a giant buffalo head. He spied an open door on the side of the large commercial glass door refrigerators holding beer and soda. The room seemed to hold a variety of guitars and what appeared to be a piano, but Jordan wasn't in the mood to explore.

"Hey, Ron!" Penny said as she moved from behind the sales counter. "I ain't seen you in a dog's age. Who is this handsome thing? Ron, you run off and get married and didn't invite us?"

"If you'd let me get a word in edgewise, I could introduce you." Turning to put one arm across Jordan's back he said, "Jordan, this ornery soul is my friend, Penny. She is the proprietor of this old rust bucket in addition to renting cabins and space for camping. I had originally reserved you a cabin so you could have your own space. Even with your truck hooked up like it was, you would have been hard pressed to endure the cold, and I figured you'd prefer to be able to take a shower every now and then."

Jordan remembered the tiny little green structures he spotted as they pulled up. Maybe that accident was a blessing in disguise. I could have made do there, though. He extended his hand. "Pleased to meet you, ma'am."

"Pleasure's mine, Jordan. Ron, take him in the back. I got a fresh batch of my special Krispy Treats cooling on top of the freezer chest."

"Not this time, Penny. I just stopped in to say hey, introduce Jordan, and pick up his deposit since he won't be needing the cabin. Tell you what. We'll take a couple to-go."

Penny walked through the small side door into the music room. She emerged moments later with four of the chocolate covered marshmallow-and-cereal looking squares in a zip-lock bag and handed them to Ron. "Y'all going up to the Mosh?"

Jordan looked at her confused. "What in the world is a mosh?"

"I told you, it's a surprise. Come on, you'll see when we get there."

As they got back in the truck, Jordan looked at the little plastic bag on the dash. "What's in the treats besides marshmallows?"

Ron laughed. "Edibles are legal out here. Penny was making those things long before the law allowed, and she still keeps them in the music room to make sure they don't fall into the hands of children."

"I don't think those will mix well with my life right now."

"Mine either. I take them to-go so her feelings aren't hurt. I haven't eaten those things in ages," Ron said as he started the truck, pulled out, and commenced to drive farther up into the foothills.

Jordan was in amazement at his beautiful surroundings. "Somehow I always pictured the Rocky Mountains as higher."

"Oh, they are. We're just in the foothills. The mountains themselves are much higher"

When they first pulled into a parking space in front of a rustic green fence bearing an antique looking sign that simply stated: Moshwhalla in large black letters; Jordan gave Ron a wide-eyed look. "This is what you call the Mosh? The guys in my group call this Moshwhalla, like the sign says! I thought they were pulling my leg. Practical jokes do run rampant in that bunch."

Ron laughed. "Well I'm glad you're happy. Between Penny and your group, my surprise was almost ruined."

They walked over to the entrance and Ron gave his name to the host, who led them to their table. It was located on a beautiful outdoor deck overlooking a slow running river and a rocky area where Jordan was amazed to see long-horned rams running up and down the steep, narrow surfaces as if they were on a wide flat road. He said as much to Ron.

"They must have known you were coming, Jordan. The mountain goats are usually hard to spot especially this close to the Pudre River."

The host got them settled with hors d'oeuvres and water. He then took their drink orders and immediately left to fill them. As the host departed, a tall, rugged-looking man in white shirt, jeans, and hiking boots walked up, a wine bottle and glasses in hand.

Ron stood to greet him. "Granger! I didn't expect to see you today." Turning to indicate Jordan, he said, "This is my client, Jordan Washington."

Jordan stood, extending his hand. "I'm happy to meet any man who comes bearing his own bottle. Please, "join us," he said, pointing to a chair.

Granger sat, placing the bottle on the table and giving each man a glass. "I like your taste in clients, Ron. I hope red wine is to your liking, Jordan." He then began pouring the wine. "Estancia Meritage is so very hard to get, but I have a friend who sends me a few bottles from time to time." He then raised his glass in Jordan's direction. "Here's to new and delightful friends."

Jordan clinked his glass to Granger's. "So, this is your place?"

"Yeah. How do you like it?

"So far, it's amazing. The view is beyond spectacular. I have friends who are dying to get tickets here. They'd come and stand on the ground like those people down there."

"Well, now you can tell them you have a friend who can accommodate you and your friends. Here is my card." Granger turned his card over and wrote another number on the back. "This is my private number. Don't share that, but you can use it to contact me anytime you want."

Jordan pocketed the card and lifted his glass. "Here's to new friends in great places."

Ron coughed and raised his glass. "Here's to old friends who are not the least bit put out by being ignored."

Granger coughed, made quick work of his wine, and suddenly rose from his chair. "Umm, I see your server is on the way with your dinner. Enjoy your meal and the show. Jordan, once again, it was a great pleasure meeting you."

Jordan smiled. "Oh, the pleasure was truly all mine."

Their meals were served, and as they ate Jordan noticed Ron was not quite as talkative as he had been. From their table overlooking the Poudre River, Jordan gave the mountain goats his full attention.

Sunset brought dessert and the beginning of the concert. Ron had still been extremely quiet through it all, and Jordan had grown weary of the whole sudden silent treatment.

"Okay, spill it."

Ron looked up. "Spill what?"

"Whatever is eating a hole in your soul at this moment. The food was great, the wine exceptional—like I-plan-to-look-it-up exceptional—and the band sounds promising. The view has been so awesome, I took pictures, and through all that greatness, I have a sulky dinner partner who arranged all this in the first place."

"I'm not sulking."

Jordan shook his head in disbelief. "Really? Your last lively moment was when your friend came over and then ran off. Of course, who could blame him with the rude way you treated him."

"The way I treated him? I didn't think the two of you even noticed I was at the damn table!"

"Whoa, slow down, Sundance. I don't know what the hell you're talking about. The man was obviously the friend who arranged our admission and this table. I may not have been here before, but I know you can't just wake up, decide to come here, and get a prime seat. I also know that usually there is a menu involved, but we had a top-shelf dinner, not to mention wine, without placing an order. If I were him, I'd reconsider the friendship, because you acted like an ass."

"So, let me get this straight. I take you out on a date, where you totally ignore me while you get damn near naked with a man you've never met before, and I was acting like an ass?"

Jordan reeled back as if he'd been slapped. He certainly felt like it. Why was Ron acting like the jealous lover? What the fuck is he— Jordan never finished that thought as the world around him turned gray, and he felt like he was trying to walk through several feet of snow.

• • •

Deejay, who had been laying quietly under the table all this time, moved to Jordan's side. He tried to put his head in Jordan's lap, but Jordan was too close to the table. Deejay looked at Ron and barked several times.

Ron quickly rose to his feet and moved to Jordan's chair..

"It's okay, boy. I got him." He kneeled next to Jordan and whispered quietly, coaxing him through the measures that had proven to calm him down effectively and to allow him to be able to take his emergency medications.

Granger came running to the table. "A customer just told me someone was having a seizure over here. What do you need, man? What can I do to help?"

"Can I use your office?"

"Sure, but this isn't a seizure. I've seen this before—this is a panic attack."

"I know, but once he's better, I'm gonna need to get him away from here."

Ron continued to coach Jordan, who sluggishly responded to his instruction. He began to count and breathe slowly. Soon he was back, and realizing where he was, tried hard to rise out of his chair and run.

"Hold on, Jordan. I've got you. We're going to move to Granger's office, where we can have some privacy and quiet."

Deejay, spotting an opening, finally moved in close to Jordan but obediently stepped to his side as Ron got Jordan to his feet. Together the group moved inside the restaurant and Granger's office.

Once inside, Granger and Ron settled Jordan on a red leather couch located along the wall adjacent to the door. Deejay moved onto the couch next to Jordan and placed his head in Jordan's lap. Jordan immediately held on to Deejay for all he was worth.

"Meds, pocket," he gasped out.

"Smart man. You brought them with you." Ron opened the bottle accepted the bottle of water Granger fetched from the small bar fridge located near the desk. He then draped the blanket he found on the arm of the couch around Jordan's shoulders.

Granger sat quietly on the edge of his desk, watching the scene unfold in front of him. "Do you guys need privacy?" he asked quietly

Ron looked up. "That would be great, if you don't mind."

Granger shook his head and moved to the door. "The light has a dimmer if that helps. Just push down on the lever next to the switch until you reach a level of comfort. I'll be at the bar if you need anything." He then left the room, closing the door firmly behind him.

CHAPTER TWELVE

Ron felt like the very ass Jordan accused him of being. What's the matter with me? I am never, ever the man who loses control. He dimmed the lights. "Jordan, is that better?" Getting no response, he moved to the couch and sat closer to Jordan, who seemed extremely focused on the fur on Deejays neck and head.

"Listen, Ron, I think the time may have come for me to find my own place to live. I can't allow or tolerate stressful issues in my life. I really appreciate the dinner and what I heard of the concert, but I can't do the stress. You have no idea, one leg or not, how bad this could have turned out for you."

Ron was stunned by Jordan's admonishment. "For me? How do you mean?"

Looking up with the glimmer of unshed tears in his eyes, Jordan said, "There is a lot you don't know about who I am and what I am capable of doing. This episode was a huge struggle for me. I have no clue how we got where we are. For that matter, where are we?"

"We're in Granger's office. I wanted to give you a space where you would have some privacy."

Jordan nodded and reached in his pocket to pull out his phone. He pressed a number and moments later began to speak "Hey,

Bish... Yeah, I pretty much feel like I sound. Do you know your way to the Mosh? ... Yeah, seriously. Can you pick me and Deejay up and put us up for a few days? ... Great. I'll meet you by the green fence. Thanks, man. ... Yeah, I'll see you then."

Ron couldn't believe his ears. "What are you doing?"

"I'm leaving your house. I'm gonna bunk at a friend's and find myself someplace convenient to live. If that takes too long, I can be put up at the VA hotel for a while."

"What about your truck? You don't need someone to come here for you. I can take you home and you can get your truck. It is yours, after all."

"I know. I'm gonna stop by and get my truck, my things, and Deejay's supplies. He and I work well together now. We'll keep our appointments at the training center." Jordan rose from the couch and stood in front of Ron. "I'd appreciate the time to pack my stuff and leave before you came home."

"Don't I get to say anything, like I don't want you to go?" Ron was devastated. This was not what he had in mind when he'd planned this night. Nope. Not what he had planned at all.

Jordan sighed hard. "I don't know where you expected this night to end up. Truthfully speaking, you might have been successful if it's what I think you were aiming at. So, this little dust-up was actually a good thing. It made me realize I'm not quite ready to be involved in a relationship. I don't have space in my head to worry about someone else's feelings. I can only worry about me right now."

Ron's frustration level was growing by the moment. He had totally lost control of things, which was more than against the grain of his personality. "Look, Jordan, like I said, I can take you home and then you can drive your truck to your friend's house."

"You don't seem to get it, Ron. I would like to do this alone and without having to rehash the night with you."

"Wait, you're leaving because of the misunderstanding we had at the table?"

"No. I'm leaving because the result of that misunderstanding made me realize that I need space and time to figure out what it is I really want for myself. I know for a fact that there is one thing I want that I can't give myself, and the man who can, will have my undying and eternal love and devotion."

"What would that be?" Ron asked. At this point he was beyond frustrated and at a loss for words.

"That's my point Ron. The man who is able to successfully meet that need will not have to be told what it is." Jordan's phone began to vibrate in his pocket. He pulled it out, and after a glance at the screen, said, "That's my ride. Thanks for everything you've done for me. I'll talk to you later." With that, Jordan picked up Deejay's leash, turned, and left the office.

• • •

Ron watched, speechless, as Jordan approached the bar, stopped to say goodbye to Granger, and then left the restaurant. He returned to the couch and just sat there with his head in his hands.

A few moments later, the door opened, and Granger walked in. This time he carried two glasses and a bottle of scotch. "I figured by the look on Jordan's face and the fact that he was leaving alone, you could probably use some of this." He poured the liquor into a glass and handed it to Ron. Pouring a glass for himself, he set the bottle down and leaned against his desk, much like he had when he was in there the first time. "What the hell, Ron? In all the years I've known you, I've never seen you act like you did tonight. You introduce the man as your client and then proceed to act like a jealous husband."

Ron took a sip from his glass. "I don't know what's gotten into me. Nah, that's a lie. Jordan has. That man has been through more than any ten men in the same period of time, and he just keeps on pushing. I never let anyone get under my skin—you know that.

Jordan was different. From the day I first laid eyes on him, I have felt drawn to him like no other man ever." He drained his glass and rose to pour himself another. "Underneath all that fire and strength is a vulnerability that just makes you want to protect him from the world."

"Does he know that you feel this way? Or are you playing the hard-to-get card?"

Ron slowly shook his head. "He doesn't know for certain, but he has an idea. That's part of why he left."

Granger stood, walked over to the couch, and sat next to Ron. "If he's as confused as I am right now, your hairy ass is screwed." Granger ticked off his points on his fingers as he spoke. "First of all, you set up this überromantic date as a surprise, if I recall correctly. Second, you introduce the man to me as your client. You could have gotten away with friend. Personally, I thought your date bailed and you brought this guy so as not to waste the night. You've done it before."

"So, is that why you began the whole flirt with him routine?"

"Slow your roll, man. I paid a little extra attention to a man who, by your behavior, was clearly not the date you set this night up for. I mean, who goes through all that trouble and then introduces him as 'my client'?" Granger asked, making air quotes. "Oh yeah, that's right, you do. Look, man. We've known each other for years. If it wasn't clear to me what the man meant to you, what do you think it looked like to him? You acted like a jackass, man, and you either got some serious groveling or growing to do. Matter of fact, make that groveling and growing."

Ron shook his head. "EJ is gonna kill me."

"EJ? Who the hell is EJ? Am I gonna need a score card to keep up with you and your men?"

"EJ is his war buddy, and his husband had to just about chain the man down since Jordan headed for Colorado." Ron stood and stumbled. "Well, driving home is out of the question."

"Damn straight. I'll put you up for the night. You can crash in here till I close. Then we'll go to my apartment and you can cry in my beer."

"Fuck you, Granger."

"Sorry, baby. I thought you knew. I don't bottom. Ever!" Laughing at his own bad attempt at comedy, Granger returned to the busy restaurant.

• • •

Later that night, Granger let Ron into the well-appointed apartment he'd built upstairs when he purchased the beautiful rustic restaurant. Ron looked around with a feeling of nostalgia. It had been a long time since he had been to one of Granger's parties here. The booze and the men flowed free, like the waters of the Poudre River. In those days, he'd had his pick of the litter.

"Reminiscing?" Granger asked as he walked into the room. He held a plate of sandwiches in one hand and two bottles of water in the other. "I got soda and water. I suggest water, but if you want soda, it's in the fridge."

Ron reached out to take the plate from Granger and placed it on the coffee table. He had always admired that table—solid oak, with a chessboard carved into one side and a storage drawer for the pieces on the other. "This thing still looks as new as the day we went to pick it up from the carpenter."

"Thanks. I try hard to take care of what's mine."

Ron picked up a sandwich half and looked at it like he had no clue what he held in his hand. "You asked if I was reminiscing. I was, but not in that 'Oh, I wish for the good old days' way. I was remembering why I gave up that life."

"It was fun." Granger laughed.

"Yeah, but it was also empty. Pretty soon the boys were as vacuous and pretentious as the nights we spent with them."

Granger and Ron ate their sandwiches in comfortable silence, and then Granger turned to look at him. "Your point is well made. That's why I stopped having them. The last one you attended was also my last."

Ron put his head down and just zoned out for a moment but recovered quickly.

"Damn, man, you still moody over that thing? When are you gonna let that go? Everything worked out. No blood was shed. Come to think of it, that explains a lot about your behavior tonight. You weren't mad—you were and are scared. You need to get honest with yourself, Ron. You want Jordan in the worst way. Don't deny it, cuz you know I can see through you."

"Well, he's gone now, so that ship has sailed," Ron said. "He's been staying with me since he got out of the hospital. We worked together to get him through the worst of the storms and the nightmares. I'm not looking forward to going home to an empty house tomorrow." Ron got up and walked to the window overlooking the Poudre River and pressed his head against the cool glass. "I gotta fix this, but I just don't know how."

"The first thing you need to do is drag your ass to the guest room and go to sleep. In the morning, avail yourself of my meditation room. Have a little talk with Jesus, man. You'll never get Jordan to forgive you until you can forgive yourself. The past is just that—past. Until you can accept that, you'll never have a future with anyone. Good night."

That said Granger strode down the hall to his bedroom.

CHAPTER THIRTEEN

As Bishop pulled into Ron's driveway, he let out a long whistle. "Damn, you were living here? You sure you want to crash at my crib? I mean, after this, it will be like moving from Buckingham Palace to a cottage in the woods."

"A cottage in the woods sounds perfect right now."

"Jordan, you look worse than you sounded, and you sounded like ten miles of bad road."

"Can we just get my shit and get out of here? We can talk later."

"Did he hurt you or something? 'Cause all I gotta do is make one call and the whole group—"

"No!" Jordan shouted. "It's nothing like that. Just back down, Bishop. I'm running on fumes right now."

"Okay, man. Just tell me what you need me to do."

"If you get Deejay's stuff from the kitchen and the family room, I'll pack what I need right away. I can get anything else later. I don't want to crowd you out, and I've accumulated a lot of stuff since I been here."

They worked in efficient silence, and thirty minutes later, the two trucks made their way west to Bishop's apartment.

By the time they got there, Jordan's pain was physical and

emotional. He'd been wearing the new prosthetic for hours, he was hung-over from his emergency meds, and all he wanted was sleep. He slowly made his way out of the truck, grateful he had packed a small bag with his immediate needs. He let Deejay out of the back seat, ensured the lock was secure on his wheelchair in the truck bed, and made his way over to Bishop, who was unlocking the door.

"Listen, I'm tired, my leg hurts, and we have group tomorrow, during which I'm going to have to tell this whole thing, so can you wait until then?"

Bishop nodded slowly. "Okay, man. Let's get you and Deejay settled. Go on inside. I'll get your crutches and Deejay's things. The door to the backyard is through the garage. I can let Deejay out if he'll let me."

"Thanks, but when I'm like this, the only people he'll allow to lead him away from me are Ron or one of the trainers. It's like that in case of an emergency and he needs to protect me. He won't bite and you can touch me, as you saw, but he won't leave my side."

"Damn, I want to get a dog like that. He is really well trained."

"You don't!" Jordan shouted. "And I hope to fuck you never need to."

Seeing his master angry again and shouting, Deejay let out a warning growl and placed himself between Bishop and Jordan.

Bishop put his hands up in surrender. "Okay, okay. Sorry. I know better than to poke the bear. I just wasn't thinking. Call off Cujo, please. Hey, Deejay. It's me, Bish. Your master's gonna be all right. Let's just get him into the house."

Jordan took a deep breath. *I need to calm the fuck down before I can't. Bishop is only trying to help and lighten the mood. The man drove I don't even know how far to come get me and lead me here. Settle down, Jordan, or they're gonna put your ass in the looney bin.*

"Nah, man, I'm sorry. Once I take off Deejay's harness, he'll settle down too. We've had a long day."

"It's cool. Like I said on the phone—same church, different pew. God's got your back, the group has your back, and I know you know I've got your back. Whatever it is, we'll all see you through it."

"Thanks. Now, I need to let Deejay off the leash."

Together they continued through the front door of the bungalow. As Jordan entered, his first thought was the outside, while beautiful, was deceiving. The entry gave way to an open floor plan that terminated in a well-appointed kitchen with gleaming counter spaces that included a stainless gas stove fit for a gourmet chef. The dishwasher, refrigerator, and appliances were all in the same stainless steel. The living and dining area were similarly spotless and decorated in modern minimalist design, one that Jordan was quite the fan of.

"Wow, this is truly up my alley. When I get my place, I'm coming to you for decorating help."

Bishop laughed as he led Jordan and Deejay through the house to the garage door entry at the back of the kitchen. When they opened the door and let Deejay out, Jordan noticed that he had been dispensed into what had to be the world's largest dog run. Confused, he turned to Bishop for an explanation.

"What? I wasn't kidding when I said I wanted a dog. I have been looking at the shelters, and I will adopt one as soon as I find the perfect fit."

"You should check with Ron. Not all of his dogs pass muster, and he allows them to be adopted. He is pretty strict, but I can't see him having a problem at all with this setup."

"Come on inside. I left the doggie door unlocked. Deejay will find you when he's done, of that I'm certain. Let me show you your room."

As they walked down the hall, Jordan couldn't hold back anymore. "Okay, you rob a bank? Rich aunt die and leave you a fortune? You and I get our benefit checks at the same rank and rate. How the hell do you afford this place?"

Laughing, Bishop opened a door on his left. "This is my office," he said as he led Jordan into a spacious room with built-in polished walnut bookshelves and a beautiful matching walnut desk. He walked over to a bookshelf and removed a photo album. "I keep this, so I never forget how I started." He opened the album to photos of the bungalow when it really was just a bungalow.

Jordan was amazed at the photo of a house that looked like the only thing he would have done was burn it down and start over.

"I know what you're thinking. I bought the house because of the land. I then tore the whole thing down and dug a new foundation. My father, brothers, and cousin worked to help me on weekends. They'd bring their kids, and we would pay the little ones a nickel a nail to make sure all the stray nails were picked up. The older kids hauled trash. I lived in the world's smallest trailer while the house was under construction. It was truly a labor of love, because in those days, I was still hypersensitive and hard to get along with. I poured all my savings and every dollar I received into this. It took two years to get it to what you see today. The guest room, my office, and the bathrooms were the last to be done. All except my bathroom, of course. My bedroom and en suite were the first to be finished so I could move out of the god-awful trailer."

Jordan flipped through the pictures. It was amazing. "All of these aren't your house."

"No. That book is the legacy record. See, in our family, it's a tradition. We buy the world's worst rat trap on the biggest land lot for next to nothing. Then as a family, we build the house. This way we can have so much more than we would have afforded outright. I remember when I was the little one, picking up the nails for my parents, aunts, and uncles. The house I best remember is my uncle's. He was a senior master sergeant in the Air Force. During the last years before he retired, he moved into the dorms on base while we built his house. Back then the wage was a penny a nail. I learned from that age the value of saving every dime for what you want."

"Yeah, I get it. I saved everything I made too. I stayed in the dorms, forewent the fancy cars and such. At the time my partner, Michael, and I were saving for our own dream home."

"Oh, man, don't tell me the family—"

"No," Jordan said, shaking his head. "They tried, but we had named each other as sole beneficiaries in the event something happened. Banks are really strict about that kind of thing. His brother, David, made sure I had a death certificate by telling his folks he wanted one. That way my savings were protected. I closed the account and put the money in new accounts till I'm ready to settle down. I'm glad David was there. I was too messed up to make real sense of anything. I owe that brother for real."

They were interrupted by Deejay's arrival. Jordan scratched his ears. "Well, you look satisfied. What do you say we get you some water and hit the hay, huh, boy?"

"Sounds like a good idea. Why don't I show you to your room? I'll bring your stuff in. Your room has an en suite, so if you want to go ahead and catch a shower, your stuff will be on the bed when you get done."

With that said, Bishop led the way down the hall and opened the door to a room as beautifully appointed as every room Jordan had seen so far, with soothing colors, masculine furniture, and a minimalist design. Jordan wasted no time heading to the chair to remove his prosthetic leg. As first days went, this one wasn't horrible, but his leg was still a bit sore.

He made quick work of shedding his clothing and hobbled his way slowly to the bathroom leaning on the furniture. He turned on the water and maneuvered into the beautiful stone tile shower stall. He almost broke down in tears when he saw the built-in shower seat. In his haste, he had not considered what he would do without his bath chair, and he was sure Bishop wouldn't think to grab it from the truck. The hot water so soothing to his tired soul and aching stump. He heard the door open and close. He finished his shower and slid back the glass door to find his crutches against the outer wall of the shower and his kit bag on the sink.

Well, scratch that prior thought. Maybe Bishop saw the chair but knew I wouldn't need it.

Jordan dried off and moved back into the room, where he found his duffel open on the chair and a pair of sleep pants on the bed. A bottle of water and two Tylenol sat on the nightstand with a note: *Sorry, we're all out of chocolates for the pillow. The management.*

Jordan took the Tylenol, finished the bottle of water, and crawled under the covers. Once he settled, Deejay took up his vigil on the floor at the foot of the bed.

"Well, Deejay, sleep tight. Tomorrow is going to be a long day."

CHAPTER FOURTEEN

Jordan was miserable. He hadn't slept well the night before, and he knew neither Dr. Mason nor Bishop was going to let him off the share hook. For that matter, the other four men in the group, who kept asking him what was wrong, were more than likely to make it the opening topic.

Sometimes group just sucks.

Dr. Mason walked into the room. "Okay, everybody, let's settle down. You guys haven't been this loud in ages. Did something phenomenal happen this weekend?"

Greg, a young vet who still had a chip on his shoulder, sitting slouched in his chair, spoke up first. "Ask Jordan. Last week he was on top of the world. Today he looks like somebody stole his puppy."

"Like hell anybody is stealing Deejay," snarked Fred. "That horse will eat 'em first."

"Speaking of Deejay," said Jason, timidly. "He usually greats everybody before he settles at Jordan's chair. Look at him."

Everyone looked at once. It was then that Jordan realized he had been reflexively stroking the head in his lap.

"Good observation, Jason. What's going on, Jordan? Because

Jason is right. Deejay is on high alert, and he hasn't been like that in a long while."

Jordan took a deep breath and relayed the details of his weekend. When he was done, he steeled himself for the onslaught he knew was coming. His was a hard group. If it was round, red, and grew on a tree, they called it an apple. They were quicker to call bullshit on something you said than any other group of men he knew. At the end of the day, they were also the only men he felt he could be real with. These men understood what he had been through. Together they had walked one another through some of the deepest valleys in emotional existence.

Once again, Greg was the first to speak up. "Ah, man, you gotta be fucking kidding me. I'm outta here."

"Jealous much?" snapped Bishop. "Sit yo angry ass down. You know you ain't going nowhere."

The cacophony of *yeahs* and *that's rights* raised the noise level in the room to unbearable.

"Okay, guys, you know the rules. Every man gets his say, but one at a time. So, Greg, since you're standing, you have the floor."

"I don't know that I would say I'm jealous, but I can't believe this bitch. Most of us would give a nut to have half of what he has. Serious truck, million-dollar dog, hot man who takes him to places with a two-year waiting list. Fuck, you ain't even gotta push your own wheelchair. Just press buttons."

"Yeah, but would you be willing to pay the total price he paid to have all that? Because it seems to me the price has been kinda high," Bishop asked.

"Still," said Greg. "The dude doesn't sit in this group every week. He doesn't know what's walking around in that thick head of yours. I bet you didn't go home every week saying, 'guess what I talked about in group.' I know without asking you never told him how you feel. Sure, you told him about your ex-partner. That shit's easy. How about the Don't Ask, Don't Tell footlocker and how it really felt when your friend—EJ, was it?—left, and your team members had to report back to duty, and the men in your dorm were shitting on you because they had no idea what all you'd been through." Greg started pacing the circle, then turned back toward Jordan. "Damn, man. According to your story, you just jetted, even though he apologized. I mean, everybody acts like an ass sometimes. You want someone to understand your angry ass, don't you? You even got your dog all nervous. You need to give me that damn dog. I'm still waiting for mine."

Jason threw a stuffed puppy at Greg "Stop whining, motherfucker. Here's your damn dog."

Jason's antic broke the tension in the room. Even Jordan began to laugh.

Once they settled back down, Dr. Mason spoke quietly into the room. "Jordan, you know there's no judgement in this room, and that goes for me as well. The thing is, you have to try to walk your way through events and see why you're really angry. So, what really set you off? Because that sounds like you had a huge anxiety attack."

Jordan felt like he was going to cry, again. He leaned forward, his head down, his arms on his knees and gave a quiet, "Down," command to Deejay, who whined and lay at Jordan's feet. "The weekend was intense but, it was the best I'd had since I returned to the States. On the way to the Mosh, he stopped and introduced me to his friend.. You guys should have seen our table. It was amazing, and the view was perfect. I guess the moment hit when his friend came over with this expensive bottle of wine and Ron introduced me as his client."

"Were you expecting him to say something else like 'this is my date'?" asked Jason.

"I would have been satisfied with 'this is my friend.'"

"That is cold," agreed Greg. "I gotta admit, I'd have lost my shit after that too."

"No," said Jordan. "That's not it. When Granger started talking, I was the only one responding. Ron got pissed because he felt ignored. I tried to talk it out, but everything just went black. I'm not ready to handle the conflict of a relationship, and I told him that."

Fred stood. "I call bullshit, man. If he hadn't called you a client, I bet you would have made sure he was included in the conversation. You do it here, Jordan. Every time somebody monopolizes the conversation, you pull Jason or one of the other quiet ones into the mix."

"I gotta agree," Bishop said. "If things had been smooth, you'd have walked in here singing 'I Shot the Sheriff' at the top of your voice. Hey, mi casa es su casa for as long as you need, but you should talk it out with your man."

Every head in the room was nodding in agreement.

Jordan looked at Dr. Mason. "You agree with them?"

"It doesn't matter if I agree with them or not. I will say we have agreed in this room that everyone would sleep on a matter before making life-altering decisions, and it doesn't seem that you did that. So the real question is, do you agree with the group?"

"I guess I do. Problem is, what do I do now?"

"Take a nap, crazy ass," said Fred. "No more decisions till you get some sleep, and then consider what you really want. From this side of the room, you want it both ways, and that's not going to work. You're either willing to try the relationship thing, or you're not. The choice is yours. But you better decide quick before the friend you're always complaining mom's you to death comes riding up here from New York on his white horse to drag you home with him."

"Yeah," Bishop said. "So you can really be Manny's big brother."

Once again, the room erupted in laughter.

"Okay, everybody. So much for Jordan. Let's make a quick go round the circle and have everyone else check in."

When the meeting finally came to a close, Jordan approached Greg. "What's the story on you and getting a support dog?"

"The problem is, I don't just want a dog. I want a trained dog. I don't have the resources, and the VA isn't being as much help as I would like."

Jordan took out his wallet and pulled out a business card. "I don't know why Dr. Mason hasn't done it but talk to Ron. He may be able to help you."

"I love you, man, but sometimes you can be so naïve. You do realize Ron's dogs don't come free or cheap, right? I'm not rated one-hundred percent like you. There are limits, and I can't afford to make up the difference."

"Call him. Tell him I gave you his card. Tell him your story. He is particular about his animals, so you have to be prepared to attend clinics with him and his staff and show you won't mistreat the dog. Like you said, he ain't cheap, and that allows him to be very picky. It also allows him to be generous. So. Call him."

For the first time since Jordan met the man, Greg smiled. He held out his hand to Jordan. "Thanks, man. I will."

Just then, Bishop walked up. "Will you ladies kiss and make up or whatever? I'm hangry, and I bet Deejay could use some water and a snack."

Jordan laughed. "I better go get the animals fed. See you later, Greg. Maybe at clinic."

"Yeah, man. Maybe at clinic."

With that, the men parted ways, with Jordan and Deejay moving toward his truck, where an impatient Bishop stood waiting.

CHAPTER FIFTEEN

"What do you mean, you don't know where he is?"

"EJ, are you even vaguely aware that Jordan is a grown man? What was I supposed to do? Maybe I should have handcuffed him to his bed? Oh wait. He left before I got home. A friend from his group picked him up. They came here and packed his stuff and Deejay's equipment, toys, and food. He took most of it with him, and they left before I got here. I recall a story about you and Dale. Didn't you go into an irrational rage because you thought he and Teddy set you up? Not to mention hiding from everyone, including your parents, for over a month? No judgement, man, but try to remember these things and give Jordan some space."

"So, what are you going to do?"

"I don't really know. Let me ask you something. What is the one thing Dale can give you that you can't give yourself?"

"I can't tell you that."

"Why not?"

"If I recall correctly, it was the one thing he said was missing from his relationship with Michael. Because of that, he was afraid the relationship would fail one day and said they would never adopt children until that was resolved between them. I'm sorry, man, but you're gonna have to put your heart on the line and figure it out."

The conversation went quiet for a moment as EJ responded to something little Manny was asking him. Then there was a voice that could only be Dale taking the phone from EJ.

"Hey, Ron. Is EJ giving you the third degree?"

"Yeah, but it's all right. That's what friends do."

"Listen. I spoke to Dr. Mason, because it was that or sedate EJ and tie him to the bed to keep him in New York. He said that I could tell you that Jordan is safe and doing okay. He knew you'd worry."

"Thanks to both of you. Listen, what is—"

"I know what you're going to ask me, and I agree with EJ. If you want to know the answer, you're going to have to put your heart on the line. Ron, I know you better than anyone, except maybe Granger, and I know you're scared. It's a bit far to travel, but if you want to work through your demons over the phone, we can. I will tell you, it's time to let that go. You'll never trust a relationship if you don't. Embrace those things that were good and let them become a part of the man you show Jordan. Throw the rest in the emotional trash and get on with that part of your life."

"Thanks, man. Listen, I've gotta go. I have a new client to see, and if he shows up, Jordan has clinic tomorrow with Deejay. We were supposed to go to the airport and walk Jordan through the crowds."

"Don't change the program. Let him tell you if he's not ready. You don't help him by treating him like he's made of sugar-glass, and you're likely to piss him off again."

"True. Well, thanks. I'll talk to you guys later."

Ron hung up the phone and wandered through the empty house. Suddenly, it seemed so much bigger, and the echo of his steps on the polished wood so much louder. His friends were right. He needed to be honest with himself first. Nothing else would do for Jordan. He had an idea of where to start, but first he had some phone calls to make.

Later that evening, Ron drove down to Vincent's. He hadn't been there in a long while, and he was hoping to just spend some quiet time listening to the music and enjoying the view. Much to his surprise, Benny and Poochie were there.

Just goes to show you, there is an owner for every dog.

Poochie was one of his dogs who just couldn't cut the service dog mustard for his PTSD clients. That didn't stop her from being not only the cutest dog ever, but the perfect fit for Bennie, a vet who suffered seizures as a result of a traumatic brain injury. Through some amazing miracle, Poochie could tell when Benny was about to have a seizure. She barked and nudged him to get to a safe place, preventing injury that could occur if Benny hit his head on a hard surface, like the sidewalk.

"And here they are, folks, the match made in heaven."

Benny and Poochie walked over to join Ron as he was about to sit at what he had come to consider his table. "Hey, Ron. I thought you were doing intense training with a new vet? Troy said he was injured on the way here in a car accident."

Ron could only shake his head. "You guys gossip like old ladies. His name is Jordan, and he's doing fine." He looked down as a paw touched his knee. "Well, hello, Poochie. I see your training is doing as well as ever."

"Hey, don't dis my dog. She may not be able to intervene or whatever with anxiety-driven clients, and she is probably a little too friendly, but she is the absolute perfect dog for me. She and Mikey make my world one-hundred percent complete."

Ron could tell from the look on Benny's face as he mentioned his husband that this was no mere statement but a fact he counted on every day.

"Benny, do you mind if I ask you a question?"

Just as he asked, Angel, Vincent's waitress, walked out with a beer for Ron, a Coke for Benny, and water for Poochie. "Anything else, guys? I'd stay and get in your business, but it's date night and I need to get home on time."

Both men indicated they required nothing else, and Angel moved on, checking the other tables.

Ron couldn't help but think *Thank God*. Normally he enjoyed Angel's patter, but tonight he was on a mission.

Benny was the first to break the silence. "So, what did you want to ask?"

"Why?"

"Well, because if you don't ask your question, I can't answer it."

Ron took a long pull from his beer. "No. I meant, why does Mikey make your world one-hundred percent complete?"

"Well, Ron, like most military, you know that I am hell bent on being independent. I may be a gay man and a bit of a twink at that, but I am still a man. The same goes for Mikey. No, he's not military, but he's a very proud black man and a father. It's tough being all that and a husband too. We give each other wings to fly, knowing the one will be there to catch the other should he fall. We'll hold each other up until our wings are strong enough to fly again. Mikey might worry about me, but he doesn't roll me in bubble wrap and lock me in the house. He trusts that Poochie will do her job, and I'll let him know when my wings give out." Benny looked at his watch. "Oh, man, I gotta get home. Listen, that was a strange question. Are you okay?"

Ron stood, drop a couple dollars on the table for Angel, and then reached out to give Benny a hug. "I am much better than I was before I got here. Thanks, Benny. Tell Mikey I said hey." With that, Ron walked away whistling. The answer had been there all along, as plain as the nose on his face. Now he just had to figure out how to show Jordan.

CHAPTER SIXTEEN

Ron was seriously frustrated. He had sent numerous texts and countless unanswered calls with as many unreturned voice messages. He thought he had made the perfect plan: take Jordan out on a date, or as many dates as it would take, and do some old-fashioned wooing. Two weeks later and he was still in the same place—nowhere. It was time to up his game and get help.

For the first time, Ron was the one initiating this conversation. He knew, though, if anyone could help him, it would be EJ and Dale. He waited patiently as the phone rang.

"Hello. Who's speaking?" asked a child.

"Hi, Manny. It's Uncle Ron. Are your daddies at home?"

"Dad says it's umpolite to not to say 'how are you' first, Uncle Ron. You're supposed to say, 'Hi, Manny. How are you?' Didn't your daddies teached you that?"

Just as Ron was about to reply, he heard the voice of an adult through the phone. He loved Manny dearly, and he even wanted to have his own child one day, but today he really needed to stick to the plan at hand. As his grandfather would often say, daylight was wasting.

"Hey, Ron." EJ's voice finally came through the phone. "Sorry about that. We're teaching Manny phone manners, and we figured the house phone is safest, since most people call our cell phones. Only family uses the house phone, and you, of course. So, what's up?"

"I need help. Jordan isn't responding to my calls and texts. I can't exactly tell him how I feel if he's not listening."

"What is it you think I can do that you haven't done? Whenever I talk to him, he says I make sense, but it seems he hasn't made any moves forward otherwise."

Ron began to wonder if even his new plan would work. "Do you know how to reach his friend Bishop?"

"Are we forming a coalition now?" EJ asked, laughing. "Yes, I know how to reach Bishop. What's he got to do with this?"

"Lately they seem to travel together when they go to group."

"You do know stalking is a criminal offense," EJ said dryly. "You get your crazy ass locked up, I'm not bailing you out."

"EJ! Please be serious."

"Wow. Stressed much?"

"Yes. Since he left, my life just feels upside-down. I know this is fast, but I've come to care for him a great deal, and I just want the chance to show him."

"You know, for the longest time, people were saying Dale and I should put our story in one of those romance novels because we came together so fast. You know how it goes. Boy meets boy, they fall instantly and madly in love, they get married, adopt a kid, and live happily ever after. Yada, yada, yada."

"Truthfully," Ron said, laughing. "You guys did give new meaning to the phrase instalove. I heard that for a while, there was a betting pool on how long you guys would even last."

"Okay, okay. So enough about me. What do you need from me to help you?"

"Call Bishop. Get him to make sure he drives down Highway 287 through downtown Loveland to get to group on Monday."

"Lucy! You got some 'splaining to do," EJ said in the worst Ricky Ricardo imitation ever.

"Well, since he won't read my texts or voicemails, I'm going to send him a message that will make my intentions clear and be impossible to ignore."

"Like all desperate plans, this one has a hitch. Supposed Bishop refuses to cooperate?"

"Oh, this is one message he is sure to get. And if it fails, I will have tried everything I can do."

"Okay, man. Well, hold on. I can at least let you know if Bishop is willing to help."

Ron could hear EJ talking in the background even though he couldn't make out the words. He must have been able to reach Bishop because he's been on the phone a long time. In an amount of time that seemed like forever, EJ ended his call and returned to the house phone, where Ron waited impatiently.

"Okay, looks like part one of your plan is going to work. Bishop loves the idea. He seems to think he knows what you're up to and thinks it will work. He said to tell you he will do his best to make sure of it. What the hell can you make happen on 287 that's got you hopeful and Bishop giggling like a sixth grader?"

"You know how to use Google?"

"Yeah, but what does Google have to do with this?"

"Think about it. I gotta go. I've got calls to make."

Ron never moved so fast in his life. When he was done, he'd spent a ridiculous amount of money. *If this works it will be worth every penny. If not, it will be the most expensive lesson I'll have ever learned since the disaster at Granger's.*

That thought brought back memories that he'd rather forget. Turnabout was fair play, though. *I wanted to know about Michael, and I promised to return the favor. Okay, Ron. In for a penny, in for a pound.* Nothing left to do but see what Monday brings.

CHAPTER SEVENTEEN

"Jordan! What's got you dragging your tail this morning? I told you I wanted to leave early today."

"Why? You never want to leave early."

"I told you that too. I have a stop to make, and I want to have time for Murphy's law to take effect and there to be some snag or another."

"Okay, okay, skip the speech. I'm ready."

As Bishop drove the familiar route, Jordan continued to look at the mountain scenery. He couldn't believe how beautiful and peaceful it was. Every weekend, he and Bishop had gone looking for what Bishop called the right piece of property for him to start constructing his forever home. He wanted an area like Ron's—lots of land for Deejay to run free, and plenty of room for guests so Dale and EJ could visit and bring Manny, as well as any other children they adopted.

"Hey, Bish. You want to have kids one day?"

"Huh? Where'd that come from? Let me tell you right now. We are great friends, but I'm not getting you pregnant."

Jordan laughed. "Ass. I'm talking about kids of your own. You know, by a surrogate or adoption."

"I don't think I've given any thought past getting a dog. I guess I figured raising me and a pup would be sufficient."

"Not me. I want kids. I'd prefer to use a surrogate, but I hear that can be dicey in the real world. While I was overseas, there was a story on the Far East Network news about a gay couple who hired a surrogate. They paid all her hospital bills and living expenses. Before she gave birth, her pastor told her she would be supporting sin if she gave her baby to the couple. She told the couple she changed her mind, she was keeping the baby, and she expected them to pay child support. When I left, they were still battling that thing out in court."

"That sucks," Bishop said as he made the turn onto Highway 287. When they reached the heart of the downtown area, Bishop pulled the car over to the curb.

Jordan stared in utter disbelief at the enormous heart outside a Loveland stationary store. The heart usually advertised the variety of Loveland souvenirs and sundries sold inside. Not today. Today, the sign, in all it's red and white glory, said:

Jordan, I promise to catch you if you fall. Ron.

Bishop jumped out of the truck, his phone in hand. "Oh, the guys are gonna just love this."

Jordan, on the other hand, was speechless. He just sat there staring and not caring who saw the tears flowing down his face.

Bishop walked back over to the truck.

Jordan looked up and asked the only question on his mind. "Did you know about this?"

Bishop shook his head. "I knew he was up to something. I agreed to make sure we took 287 through Loveland and you were in the passenger seat. Not in a million years could I have come up with this. I thought maybe one of those little hearts on the light posts. But this..." he said, waving his hand toward the heart-shaped marquee sign. "This is above and beyond anything I would have thought of."

While they sat there, talking through the window a passerby stopped and took pictures of the elaborate sign. One man asked, "Do you guys know Ron and Jordan?"

Jordan shook his head no. Bishop nodded.

The man approached Bishop and gave him a business card. "If Jordan ignores this, give Ron my number. I'd gladly fall for a man like that sight unseen."

Jordan looked at the man like he had two heads. "Why?"

"Because any man who would go so far as to put his heart literally out on main street will do anything to make his man happy. I'd give my eye teeth to the recipient of that kind of devotion. You guys tell Jordan he's a lucky man. If he turns Ron down, tell him I said thank you."

Jordan reached over to Bishop and took the business card. Handing it back to the man, he said, "Well, you might as well take this back, because Ron is off the market."

He turned back to Bishop in time to hear him say into his phone, "Seriously, man. I got pictures!"

As Bishop got back in the truck, an older man came running from the store, waving an envelope. "Hey, wait! Are you Jordan?"

Jordan looked at the little man huffing and puffing from his short run. "Yeah, I'm Jordan."

"I'm sorry," he said. "I almost missed you. Ron asked me to give this to you if you stopped long enough to look at the sign."

Jordan accepted the envelope and thanked the shopkeeper. He opened the envelope as an apologetic Bishop put the truck in gear and headed for the counseling center. Inside was a plain note card.

If you are reading this, I hope it means you have decided to take a chance on what we can have together. If you have, please text me your address and allow me to take you out on a proper date this Friday night.

It was signed simply *Ron*.

Jordan folded the note and put it back in the envelope before securing it. He stayed silent as he pulled out his phone and began to type. Bishop said nothing as he navigated the streets to get them to group. Jordan liked that he could trust Bishop to let the quiet be without being told. He always just knew.

Group went by fast. Bishop decided not to share his pictures with the group, which made Jordan wonder who he had talked to on the phone. Greg was absent, and that alone decreased the amount of time to get to each member. For the first time since he had started working in the group, Jordan asked to use an opt-out chit, meaning he didn't want to share that day. No one asked any questions and let him be. He knew he would pay the price next week. He and Greg would be center stage for sure, unless someone had something they desperately needed to work out.

The ride home was again quiet, until they pulled into the driveway. Bishop turned to Jordan. "I've left you in peace ever since we saw the marquee and you got Ron's note. I just need to ask. Are you okay, man? Because you're starting to scare me. You know it's not good for us to be silent and inside our own heads for too long. When we do, things go boom, and I really worked too hard on my house to see it go up in flames."

Jordan let out a slight laugh. "I'm fine. I'm about to make a life-altering decision, and I need the quiet to think it through."

"Life-altering? Did the man ask you to marry him or something? I mean, I know you guys went through something, but let's not get overdramatic here."

Jordan got out, let Deejay out, and walked around to the front of the truck to lean on the hood as he spoke. "I realize that, but the statement he put on his message means he's figured out something extremely important to me. I once told him the man who could give me the one thing that I couldn't give myself would be the recipient of my undying love and devotion. The problem is, he's figured out what it is and he knows what it means to me. I don't want him looking at a relationship with me with expectations that I might not be able to meet at this time. It's one of the reasons I didn't take his calls."

Bishop shook his head and proceeded to unlock the door. Once inside, he unlocked the doggie door to the yard for Deejay. When Jordan finally joined him, Bishop put both hands on his shoulders and looked deep into Jordan's eyes.

"Here me out because these emotional extremes have got to stop. Man up! Stop whining and tell the man what you want and need. Your friend EJ and his husband notwithstanding, love takes time."

CHAPTER EIGHTEEN

Friday came fast. Jordan stood in front of the mirror and asked Bishop, "How about this shirt?"

"It looks as good as it did after the blue one and before the red one. Didn't you say he said casual? Well, a basic black golf shirt is casual."

Just then, the bell rang.

"Well," Jordan said, "it's gonna have to be, because he's here." He moved to the foyer and opened the door. Ron stood there in a royal blue button-down shirt with the sleeve cuffs rolled up and the neck open. Jordan thought he looked as edible as his favorite ice cream sundae.

"You look amazing, Jordan. Are you and Deejay ready to go?"

Jordan bid Bishop good night and whistled for Deejay.

Bishop reached for Deejay's leash. "I have an idea, guys." He turned to Ron. "You know what to do if Jordan has a meltdown, right?"

"Of course, I do."

"Jordan. This is the man who told the entire state of Colorado that he would be there to catch you if you fall. Let him. Deejay and I will be fine."

"I don't know," Jordan said slowly. "I haven't been anywhere without Deejay since we partnered up."

"Remember our conversation when we got home Monday, Jordan? Well, it's time to cowboy up, man."

Jordan looked at Ron for some sign of confirmation.

"It's up to you. Do what's gonna make you feel the safest."

Jordan turned to Deejay and said, "You be a good boy and obey Bishop. I'll be back."

Deejay whined as if to disagree.

Jordan stepped out the door to join Ron, who was standing at the truck, holding his door open. Once Jordan got in and got settled, Ron closed the door and hopped into the driver's seat.

As they set off, Jordan asked, "Where are we going?"

"I'm taking you to my favorite place. I go there when I want to think. I sometimes bring camping gear and spend the night, especially over the Fourth of July holiday. I'm not a fan of the fireworks."

Ron made a turn onto a road Jordan was certain he would never have found even in broad daylight. They continued to move up the mountainous road until they came to a beautiful clearing. As Jordan got out of the truck, he was awestruck. The sky was clear, and the stars were amazing.

"I can see why this is your favorite place."

"It actually abuts a semi-rugged campground. I thought you would appreciate it. There are cabin-like structures farther out. Nothing fancy. Basically, it's shelters for the hikers and nature lovers who know when they get up here, they won't want to hike back down again." As Ron spoke, he moved to the back of his truck and pulled out a thick blanket and a large cooler.

"Here," said Jordan. "Let me give you a hand. I can't believe this. A picnic dinner under the stars?"

"What? Not cool?"

"Actually, very cool," Jordan said as he worked to spread out the blanket.

Once they got situated, they sat and ate the most amazing spread Jordan had seen. Roast beef sandwiches, potato salad, and barbeque kettle chips, with cheesecake for dessert and a bottle of Estancia Meritage.

"Wow. You put a lot of work into this. All my favorites."

"Well, dig in, 'cause the only waitstaff out here is us."

The two of them were never big on talking while eating. Tonight was no different, but Jordan could tell there was something heavy on Ron's mind. He'd been around the man long enough to know, and a few weeks away wasn't going to change that.

"I'm not going to bite you, Ron," Jordan said. "I can tell you have something serious on your mind."

Nodding, Ron look in Jordan's eyes. "I wanted you to see this place, like I said. I also wanted to be someplace where I could share some things with you without the risk of being interrupted." Ron went back to the truck and got some pillows out that looked like they truly had seen better days. "I use these when I stargaze," he said, by way of explanation.

"That truck bed is starting to look like the proverbial clown car. What else you got in there?"

"Let's just sat I come prepared for a variety of eventualities. The weather around here can turn on a dime, and sometimes I have just needed to get away for a day or two."

Jordan nodded. "I can relate to that. So..." He made himself comfortable. "What did you want to tell me? I do remember you owe me, as I did tell you about Michael."

"It was really hard for a while to figure out what I could possibly give you that you couldn't give yourself. You are so strong and determined. You managed to push through everything life threw at you. Even as I came to understand that the strongest of men still need someone to have their back, it was hard to see myself as the person you could accept as that man."

"Why?" Jordan asked in a voice so quiet, he could barely be heard.

"That's what I brought you up here to tell you."

CHAPTER NINETEEN

As Ron settled in to tell his story, he realized this was as much for him as it was for Jordan. Granger was right. It was time to let go of the mistakes of the past.

"When Granger first took over the Mosh, the place was little more that the small stage and a concession stand. He got the idea to build a restaurant-slash-sports bar as a way to have the place function year-round, except when the snows make travel dangerous. This winter was mild, but don't get used to it. Your truck will earn its keep next year, I can assure you.

"Anyway. His other grand idea was to build the ultimate apartment above the restaurant. We weren't into BDSM per se, but we considered ourselves kinky and invited like-minded men to some of the most elaborate sex parties in the universe. Those parties were a man buffet, and I'd happily had my fill. It was all consenting adults, or so we thought until one really bad night.

"A young man named Sam began coming to the parties with his friends. He was cute and claimed to be into the same scene as everyone there. Granger brought him over to meet me. By then I was beyond high and I should have gone home. Sam said he wanted to be the meat in a man sandwich. Something about him bothered me on a level I couldn't define but, between the booze and the drugs, I was more interested in listening to my dick than my brain. We all went to Granger's room and we got his safeword, plus gave him a bell ring in case his mouth was busy. I will spare you the details, but when we were done, he went out and continued to party with his friends.

"He kept coming back to the parties, and after a while, he and I developed an exclusive relationship outside the party scene, or so I thought. We'd stopped attending the parties and instead spent weekends together. We never saw each other during the week. I wasn't being very smart back then, and it never occurred to me to ask what he did for a living. I believed our relationship was growing. I decided I was in love with him and planned to tell him so when he came over Presidents' Day weekend. The problem was, he begged off that weekend, explaining he had something important to do with his family.

"An acquaintance told me about a party at Granger's that was going to be happening that Sunday night. I didn't party during the week because, like most poor and obscure people, I had to get to work the next day and hangovers were not acceptable. Monday was a holiday, so I decided to go to Granger's and at least hang out for a while.

"When I got there, one of his friends asked me if I wanted to party. I declined, and in anger, he wanted to know how it was everyone wanted his friend but not him. He laughed, called me a fool, and said his friend was off partying as the meat in a man sandwich, while I was sitting here protecting my virtue. He said if I didn't believe him, to go take a gander in Granger's bedroom.

"I couldn't believe what I saw next. Granger and another man, John, were spit-roasting the little mother fucker. When I demanded to know what the fuck was going on, everything stopped. I grabbed Sam by the throat and threw his naked ass out the apartment. At first Granger and John both thought I had lost my mind. All unattached men were fair game, and apparently Sam had continued to attend the weekday parties with his friends. I went outside, slapped him, and told him I never wanted to see his whoring ass again. Talk about the pot accusing the kettle.

"The next day, I found Sam trying to hang himself in my backyard. Fortunately, I got home just in time to see him as he took the leap off the lowest branch of the tree that grew outside my bedroom window. I went through the window and jumped to the branch, adding my weight to his. The branch broke, sending me and Sam to the ground. We hit hard, and I broke both legs because of the way I landed."

"Sam's family committed him to a private psych hospital, but not before he told everyone who would listen that Granger and I took advantage of him. He claimed we lured him into the bedroom and gave him no way to out, then whored him out to John. He said he wanted to die because he couldn't face the shame. He chose my backyard because he wanted me to feel guilty for what I caused him to become. His parents raised hell and demanded the police be involved. We were all charged with rape, and I was charged with assault for the way I threw him out of the apartment and slapped him. Granger's father paid his bail. John and I had no such rich relatives, so my life just spiraled into the eighth level of hell."

Ron needed a break from the intensity of the conversation. He stood and began to pace up and down for a few minutes. He finally returned to the blanket and lay back down next to Jordan. He needed Jordan to see his face as he continued his story.

"Granger located Sam's friends and convinced them to testify at our trial. He would have lost the Mosh were it not for his father. I'm telling you, between Granger's family and Sam's, it was the battle of the deep pockets. John and I only benefited because we were all tried together.

"I went over the emotional deep end. I lost every dime I had paying for my defense. An ex-boyfriend testified that their relationship dissolved because of the Sam's habitual histrionics. He called Sam a nymphomaniac and the world greatest dramatic actress. We were eventually found not guilty, but I still blamed myself for not listening to the signals that told me something was wrong with that man in the first place.

"Granger was able to move on. I wasn't. I couldn't forgive myself for contributing to the destruction of a life. Because at the end of the day, no matter how crazy he was, my individual actions contributed to his ultimate end. I never went to another one of those types of parties and Granger never threw a party of any kind in his apartment again.

"I went to stay with a friend on Long Island for a while. That's when I met Dale. He had just graduated school, moved to Sayville, and was starting Chances. He slowly helped me put my life back together, get my emotional feet under me, and find a new purpose in life. He introduced me to the owners of Second Chance Service Animals, who trained me to work with older service dogs. I learned that I had a real knack with the dogs and decided to do something to give back. Hence Pawz with a Cause.

"I thought I had hurdled all this because I never let anyone get that close to me again until I met you. When Granger started flirting with you, all I could see was history repeating itself. It just didn't cross my brain that— like before— Granger had nothing telling him you were special to me. Had he known, he would have been on his best behavior. He later told me he thought my date bailed and I brought you so as not to have him lose money on the canceled table."

Ron sat up and took both of Jordan's hands in his. "I owe you the world's largest apology. I am so sorry. I wish I could say I don't know what got into me, but you know that would be a lie. I do want to get to know you in every way. I think we have the makings of a great relationship. I want to be there to soothe you when your nightmares disrupt your sleep. I want to walk with you as you gain each new success. Most of all, I want to be the man you allow yourself to be vulnerable with and to catch you if you fall."

With that, he pulled Jordan into his arms, praying that Jordan would not turn him down.

Jordan went to him willingly. The kiss they shared set Ron on fire.

CHAPTER TWENTY

Jordan lay in Ron's arms, looking up as the sky. "This has to be the most beautiful place I've been in a long time."

Ron leaned up and kissed the top of Jordan's head. "I'd like to be able to really show off and tell you which stars and planets are visible, but astronomy isn't my thing."

Jordan shivered as the air cooled.

"You ready to go back down?"

Jordan shook his head. "No. I like the peace up here. Tell me you rented one of those cabin things just in case."

"I always rent one of those cabin things just in case. Actually, I have my own permanently assigned cabin. It's something Penny does for the few locals who spend a lot of time up here."

Ron rose and extended his hands to help Jordan up. Together, they folded the blanket, repacked the cooler, and loaded everything into the truck. Once they were both secured in their seats, Ron slowly drove down a rocky road until he came to a stop in front of a structure that resembled a miniature log cabin.

Jordan looked around as they began to bring everything into the cabin. "When you said rustic, you weren't kidding, were you?"

"You hate it," Ron said.

"Actually, I think it's kind of cool. Speaking of cool, please tell me the fireplace works."

"I'll have the fire started in a few moments. Every time I come up here, the last thing I do before I leave is set up the fireplace for the next time," Ron said as he used a long matchstick to set the kindling afire.

While he did that, Jordan set the cheesecake, wine, and cups on the scarred wood coffee table. Sitting back, he realized the couch was one of those futon things and was already open and flat. "Expecting company?" he said.

"More like hoping, although to be honest, I never sit that thing up into a couch. I usually hike up here, and by the time I get here, all I want to do is fall flat on my face and sleep."

Jordan laughed. "Well, I'm not hiking up here or anywhere in the near future, so anytime I come, there will have to be trucks involved. After Iraq and other places I don't talk about at parties, my climbing days are over. I'm looking to develop new pastimes." He then poured out the wine and raised his cup. "To new beginnings."

Ron moved to the futon and tapped his cup to Jordan's. "New beginnings." After drinking from his cup, he took Jordan's from him, set them on the table, and pulled Jordan into his arms. "You have no idea how much you have already come to mean to me."

"I think the giant heart-shaped marquee spoke volumes," Jorden replied as he leaned in for a kiss.

Ron's kisses were amazing. When Ron ran his tongue over Jordan's bottom lip, demanding entrance, Jordan opened for him more than willingly. He felt like he had died and gone to heaven as Ron's tongue explored every inch of his mouth, devouring him like he was the last meal on the earth.

The need for oxygen forced them apart. Ron reached down and removed Jordan's right sneaker and sock. He then helped Jordan remove his prosthetic and began to slowly massage the stump through Jordan's jeans until Jordan stopped him.

"Keep that up and the denim is going to abrade my skin."

"Then maybe we should get the jeans out of the way," Ron said as he unbuttoned Jordan's fly and began to dispense of the interfering fabric. That done, he once again resumed his massage of Jordan's legs and stump. Then he slowly kneaded the flesh of both at the same time, advancing inch by inch until he got to the area where groin met thigh.

Jordan had forgotten how sensitive he was in that area. It had been so long, he let out a loud hiss as Ron began to alternate the pressure from his fingers with soft kisses along both sides of his groin. "Ron! Oh God!" he cried out as he reached out to touch Ron.

"Shhh, babe. Lie back. Put yourself in my hands. Let me make this good for you." Ron slid his hands up Jordan's sides, carrying the golf shirt with him until he was successful in pulling it over his head. He then commenced kissing his way back down Jordan's chest stopping when he reached the left nipple. Softly, he suckled it, alternating the sucking with biting down. He continued his abuse of the tender flesh until the dark brown nipple stood hard and erect, then commenced to give the same treatment to the right nipple.

Jordan writhed in response to Ron's ministrations. Once again, he reached for Ron. "Let me—"

"Not this time," Ron whispered as he took Jordan's hands and tenderly laced them over his head. "Relax. Fall, Jordan. I promise to catch you."

Without further protest, Jordan lay back on the couch as Ron asked.

For his part, Ron returned to his worship of Jordan's body. Tenderly, he kissed every one of Jordan's scars. He finally reached Jordan's long, engorged cock. He licked long, slow stripes all along it until, in one smooth move, he sucked the organ into his mouth.

Jordan, overwhelmed by all the stimulation, could not be still. He pushed his hips up, fucking Ron's mouth until, with a shout, he came without warning. Jordan shook from the intense sensations overcoming him as Ron swallowed and then ever so slowly cleaned the residual cum until he released Jordan's cock from his mouth. Ron moved forward and kissed Jordan, sharing his taste with him.

"I'm sorry," whispered Jordan. "I should have warned you, but I couldn't. Your mouth is dangerous."

"You're fine, and I am not finished."

"Oh God, I hope not."

Smiling, Ron pulled a box from under the couch and extracted a well-used tube of lube. Standing, he removed his clothes, and after extracting a few condoms from his jeans pocket, let his pants fall to the floor.

Jordan stared in awe as his every dream was made real in front of him. Ron's body was all Jordan imagined it would be and more. "You're beautiful!" he whispered.

"No," Ron responded as he moved his hands slowly caressing Jordan's thighs. "You're the beautiful one. He then bent down, and his lips followed his hands tenderly kissing the warm skin. "I have prayed so hard for this moment.'

Overwhelmed by the sensations coursing through his body, Jordan cried out, "Oh my God, Ron, if you don't hurry up and fuck me, I'm going to do it myself."

"As much as I'd like to see that, not this time. If you can still talk, then maybe I need to step up my game, because I am definitely doing something wrong." With that, Ron changed the angle of his fingers until Jordan's upper body curled off the bed with a loud moan. Ron moved between Jordan's legs as he donned the condom and liberally lubricated his cock. He lifted Jordan's legs against his chest and slowly entered Jordan until he was balls deep.

They began to move together in a sensuous dance that made Jordan feel like he was at first floating, then flying.

Somewhere in the distance, he thought he could hear Ron shouting.

"That's it, baby. Let go. Fly with me."

Jordan was in freefall much like his parachute jumps, he soared allowing himself to move freely on the winds of feeling and till he landed screaming with joy. When he opened his eyes again, Ron was cleaning him up. He wanted to ask where Ron got the water from, but he just didn't care. Instead, for the second time in their relationship, he decided to just be.

EPILOGUE

"Are you sure about this?" Bishop asked for the umpteenth time as he loaded the last of Jordan's things into his truck.

It had been a month since that night with Ron in the mountain cabin. Jordan had returned there twice since then, and like Ron had once done, Jordan made sure there were things up there he might need if the stay became extended: crutches, supplies for Deejay, and a much warmer blanket.

He smiled as he remembered telling Ron he was going up alone. Ron must have broken a world record getting up there before Jordan planned to go, because on the rustic coffee table lay a satellite phone and instructions on how to use it just in case.

Jordan and Deejay spent the day exploring the area. He was surprised to find it was much larger than it had looked at night. He spent the night meditating the way he'd learned from Dr. Mason. He'd had a lot to focus on as he sat on his blanket outside and considered the stars. He had a lot to forgive.

He set out the cast iron kettle he'd found in the little mom-and-pop store in Loveland where he'd gone to revisit Ron's message. He had four pieces of paper with him; each bearing one name and read off each name as he spoke to the winds.

"EJ, I forgive you for leaving me behind. It was foolish to think you could do anything but go, considering the circumstances. I am happy that the evil aimed at you was thwarted and you now have the life you deserve.

"Michael, I forgive you. I wish you could have lived to have the life of your dreams. I realize now that life would not have been with me. We were amazing friends and ride-or-die buds, but as a couple, we never would have worked. Our paths were too divergent. I hope you sleep in peace and your troubled soul has found a resting place full of all the beauty you enjoy so much.

"Ron, I forgive you. It is hard to start something new on the detritus of an unresolved past. Fear will always freeze forward movement. So, I pray you find a peace that will confound even the wisest of men."

Jordan then put the four papers in the kettle and set them on fire. He didn't need to read the fourth paper— it bore his name and he didn't need to see it to concentrate on what he needed to say.

I forgive myself. I know that this is where forgiveness truly has to begin. I have not always made the wisest decisions, but I accept that this is a part of growth and know that I will continue to make mistakes. I will endeavor to give greater thought to my actions, words, and deeds. Most of all, I will remind myself daily that despite what I've lost, I have gained so much more and live my life with an attitude of gratitude.

The papers burned to ash. and Jordan dumped the ashes in his hand and then blew them into the wind. *Give your troubles to the winds*, his grandmother had once told him.

"Okay, you tough old Seminole," he said. "I have."

"Where did you go?" asked Bishop, pulling Jordan back from his memories.

"I was just remembering my last night on the mountain."

"I still say you were crazy to go up there by yourself."

"I was safe. I had a phone and I had Deejay."

"You put way too much stock in that dog, but okay." Bishop moved to Jordan and embraced him in a tight hug. "If it doesn't work, you know where home is."

"I know that. I also know that unless I give it the try it deserves, then it's for sure to fail."

That said, Jordan secured Deejay in the back seat, climbed in his truck, and took off for home. When he arrived, he found Ron standing at the door waiting, with two wine glasses in his hands. He handed one to Jordan, then raised his glass and said, "To new beginnings."

Jordan agreed. It would be a journey, and some of it would be uphill. He wouldn't be traveling alone, though. Ron would be there to catch him when he fell.

ABOUT THE AUTHOR

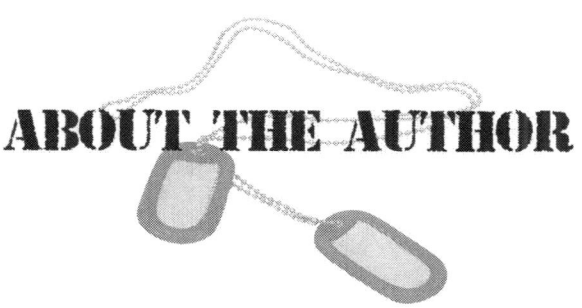

Miski Harris was born and raised in New York City with her younger brother and sister. She worked as a critical care nurse, served in the military, raised five amazing sons and traveled extensively. When Miski sets her mind to achieve something there is no force on earth that can stop her.

Through all the organized chaos that has often defined her life, her one constant has been a love of books. Reading has always been a mainstay for her, and she is rarely seen without her Nook on which she has reportedly downloaded over 2,000 novels. A woman of boundless imagination, she desires to give life to the characters who maintained residence in her imagination. With that in mind, she has finally put pen in hand to fulfill a lifelong desire to write books of her own. She published her first M/M romance novel; Don't Ask Don't Tell after a close friend and author challenged her to join the Nation Novel Writing Month initiative. At the end of that month, the first draft of her book was complete. Several edits later, Don't Ask Don't Tell made its debut on the Amazon and Kindle Unlimited bookshelves.

Ask anyone who knows Miski to use one word to describe her and they would say fierce. A prior military commander once defined her as a "tender warrior". Friends, patients, and associates have always found a strong advocate in this woman who is not afraid to speak her mind.

Miski believes three things: challenge is just another word to define worlds to conquer and lines to cross; love and faith are the most powerful forces in the universe, and the only thing that hinders success is to fail to try. With that in mind, she invites you to join her in a world where love is second to nothing and life is the greatest adventure of all.

Miski resides in Prince Georges County, Maryland coexisting with two precocious cats: Freddie and Marshall.

Made in the USA
Middletown, DE
17 November 2025